THE PEACE RIVER KID

drew with cold deliberation.
There was the report of a gun.
With a cry of mingled pain and rage
the Peace River Kid
held up a broken and mangled hand.
His gun fell into the dirt.
The other five outlaws whirled
as one man and the hands of all
slapped gunward. But their amazed
glances fell upon the smoking
weapon in Chet Kelvin's hand,
and at his crisp word of command
their hands jerked back.

OUTLAW RANCH

by Frank C. Robertson

WILDSIDE PRESS

ONE

Dust hung over the tithing corrals like fog. Four hundred head of snorting, wild-eyed cattle had been milling about there for two hours, and they had churned the dry dirt into stifling powder. But now the last bunch had been passed upon and Chet Kelvin walked away from the corrals with half a dozen sturdy Mormon ranchers at his heels.

As he passed out of the gate Kelvin looked up and grinned a friendly greeting at a sixteen-year-old lad he had previously noticed roosting on top of the fence with bland indifference to the choking dust. The boy was dressed in a brand-new cowboy outfit, but somehow his unsuppressed eagerness struck a sympathetic chord in the heart of the young cattle buyer.

"Will you men have a drink before we settle up?" Chet hospitably invited the Mormons.

There was no reply, and somewhat puzzled Chet repeated the invitation.

This time he was answered by a broad-shouldered, bearded man by the name of Carey.

"Thank you just the same, but us Mormons don't drink liquor. It's against our Word of Wisdom," he said.

"Especially when the bishop's around—an' Carey's our bishop," a brawny Mormon laughed.

"Far be it from me to ask any man to go against his principles," Chet said. "I respect yore scruples, an' admire their wisdom. But will you-all have a cigar?"

The Mormons looked at each other and grinned.

"Sorry, but smokin' tobacco is also against our religion," Carey said.

"Pardon me if I make another blunder, but would it be against yore religion if I buy each of you a lead pencil?" Kelvin asked gravely.

The Mormons laughed, but one of two young fellows who had just ridden up and were looking over the top of the corral fence from their horses' backs addressed Kelvin.

"If yo're just lookin' for somebody tuh buy drinks for, stranger, me an' my pard'll absorb a few with you."

Chet regarded the young fellows with casual interest. They were dressed as cowhands, and were gray with trail dust from their wide-brimmed hats to the ends of their tapideros. Their sweat-stained horses indicated that they had come a long way. They were young fellows, both rather good-looking, yet with a hard, daredevil look about them with which Chet Kelvin, sometimes known as "Tornado Tex," was far from being unfamiliar.

"All right, boys," the cattle buyer answered good-humoredly. "Soon as I finish my business with my friends here I'll have a drink with yuh."

"We'll be waitin'," the puncher replied, and turning their horses they rode on a gallop the short distance across to the nearest saloon.

Bishop Carey cleared his throat. "A-hem," he began dubiously. "What you do, my friend, is, of course, nothing to us. But if I were you I'd be purty careful about minglin' much with— with men of that stripe."

"That so?" Kelvin queried. "You know them?"

"No, I can't say that I do," Carey said. "They're strangers in Curryville. You've heard of the Wild Ones, no doubt?"

"Who ain't?" Chet laughed.

"You are now getting into the Wild Ones' territory," Carey said. "Many people here, if not actively in sympathy with Kirk Holliday and his men, are so afraid of them that they give them aid and sympathy. Being a cattle buyer, and traveling about the country the way you do, the Wild Ones might be interested in your movements."

"I see," Chet said gravely. He realized that Carey's warning was well meant, and probably authentic. "You mean you suspect those two punchers of belonging to the Wild Ones?"

"They might," Carey said guardedly.

"Well, thanks," Chet said. "I'll be careful."

He went into the tithing office with the men and gave them each a draft on the Idaho Land & Livestock Co. to pay for the cattle he had bought. Those drafts, good as the gold in any Western bank, were accepted without question.

His business with the Mormons settled, Chet Kelvin crossed the street and entered the saloon. Cutting and counting the various bunches of range cattle had been hot, dusty work, and he was thirsty. He had slipped over a few times before during the day, and had conversed sociably with the bartender.

As he entered he saw the two young fellows Carey had warned him against touching glasses at the bar. They set their glasses down on the bar with a crash and welcomed him with a whoop.

"Just in time tuh pay fer these here drinks," the smaller of the two shouted. "What'll yores be?"

"Beer," Chet smiled.

They drained their glasses, but before Chet could pay the puncher who talked the most threw a gold piece upon the bar.

6

"Cattle buyer?" he inquired.

"I occasionally buy up a cow here an' there," Kelvin said modestly. "Allow me to return the honors. What will it be, gents?"

"Whisky," the punchers said in a breath.

The other puncher bought, after that, and then Chet set up the cigars. By that time the two tough young punchers were beaming.

"Mister," said the smaller one, "if it's cows yo're lookin' fer you've hit a ridin' burro of information. But first off let me interduce myself. I'm Jack Fossum. The dish-faced hombre with me is called Al Biggers."

"I'm right pleased to meet you both," Chet said cordially. "I'm Kelvin—Chet Kelvin."

"Put 'er there, Chet," Biggers boomed. "Barkeep, fill up them glasses."

"You was speakin' of some cows I might pick up," Chet reminded.

"You bet," Fossum said. "The barkeep was just tellin' us you'd bought 'bout five hundred head from these Mormons. You fixin' tuh buy up a trail herd?"

"That's more or less my idea," Chet admitted. "I want to buy between two an' three thousand head for the Idaho range. They tell me these little, wild southern Utah cattle do well up there—most like the Texas longhorns."

"Yeah, these Dixie cattle are so light behind that they spend half their time standin' on their heads. But you git 'em on good feed an' tie rocks to their tails so their hind ends won't drive their horns into the ground an' they do right good," Jack Fossum said solemnly.

All three laughed, and the bartender joined in heavily.

"The only trouble is yo're on the wrong side o' the mountains," Biggers scowled. "Now if yuh had this bunch a hundred miles east o' here I could show yuh all the cows yuh'd want, an' dirt cheap, too."

"Any way to get over there?" Chet asked interestedly.

"Sure there is. You could trail what yuh've bought here over the mountains. Tell yuh what you do: You ride back over with us an' look the country over. If you don't find more cows than yuh want I'll stand the drinks," Biggers offered.

"I was figgerin' on goin' on south," Chet said. "I've got three hundred head scattered on up the country an' I figgered I could make up a herd without much trouble."

"Hey, Al, yo're forgettin' that we got business down in Pipe Springs," Jack Fossum interrupted. "We can't go back there for a week."

7

"Dang my slats, I plumb forgot that," Biggers said, and looked at the cattle buyer with regretful confusion.

"I could go on south, an' if I didn't fill my herd I might—" Chet suggested.

"No, no. I know dang well yuh kin save as much as two dollars a head, an' have an easier trail this other way," Fossum contended. "Listen, Chet, I'll tell yuh what you do. You go over an' see Hank Stevens—he's got a ranch over toward Cattle valley. You orta get two, three thousand head from him, an' he'll know just where yuh can get more if you want 'em! We work for the I X L which is 'bout fifty miles south of there. Right now we're on our way tuh Pipe Springs tuh buy some thoroughbred horses for our boss."

"Might be a right good idea," Kelvin agreed. "I'll think it over."

He had another drink with his two young friends and returned to the corrals, where the cattle he had bought were now in charge of one of the Mormon ranchers and his two sons. Chet had arranged for them to be held in the Mormon's pasture until his trail herd was made up. The animals, slim, narrow-hipped, wild-eyed heifers, were already being let out of a gate, which they approached with loud and terrified snorts, and then ran as if the devil was after them when they got through.

Good enough stuff, Kelvin thought, but he had paid a little more than he had expected to. It was his first trip to this section. The cattle grew small, but they would fatten up and grow big on the better ranges of Idaho and Montana if taken young enough.

What the two punchers had told him stuck in his memory, for all that he had no intention of following the minute directions they had given him. Those two had all the earmarks of outlaws, and he was no stranger to their ways. What they said might all have been in good faith, but, on the other hand, if he was green enough to ride the lonely trail they had outlined it would be easy for them to stage a hold-up.

He gave a few instructions to the Mormon who had charge of the cattle, and was about to start back toward his hotel when his eyes fell upon the boy he had noticed before roosting on the fence. The lad was still looking at the vanishing cattle with star-eyed interest.

"Those your cattle?" he asked eagerly.

"Yes, sonny, I reckon they are," Chet admitted.

"You must be a big cattleman," the boy said.

"No, I reckon not. Yuh see I'm just a sort o' buyer for a company up in Idaho," Chet smiled.

"Then you're a stranger here, too?"

8

"I reckon I am, son. Which way are you-all headin'?"

Unconsciously the boy lowered his voice. "I don't know," he said. "You see my sister and me are out here looking for our older brother. He owns a big cattle outfit, the I X L. It's close to a place called Highriver, because that's where he used to mail his letters. But we ain't heard a word from him for over a year, so we are on our way to find out what's happened to him."

"Then you must know where yo're goin'," Chet remarked.

"The trouble is everybody says we're foolish to go there. One man here, a Mormon bishop by the name of Carey, told us straight out that Highriver was no place for a decent girl to go, and he had the nerve to say that the I X L belonged to an outlaw named Broome, and that nobody had ever heard of my brother."

"What was yore brother's name?"

"Charles Harrison. I'm Bud Harrison, and my sister's name is Leda—that's her signaling to me now. Well, guess I'd better jump. We've bought an outfit to drive out there and see what's happened to Charley anyway. My sister is afraid he's dead. Well, so-long," the boy said.

"Just a minute," Chet murmured. "You got any idea how long a trip yo're undertakin'?"

"They say it's all of a hundred miles." Bud Harrison grinned.

"You got a guide?"

"Just an old feller to drive the team and do the cooking. He calls himself 'Nevada.' Kind of a peculiar old boy."

"You startin' right away?" Chet asked.

"Yes; I see the buckboard is all ready to start," Bud said.

"It's a kind of coincidence, but I'm headin' for that country myself," Chet drawled. "Goin' in there tuh buy cows. Likely I'll overtake you before you get there."

"That'll be fine," Bud said. "We'd be glad to have you camp with us."

As Kelvin walked toward the hotel he got a good look at a flaxen-haired, sweet-faced girl of about twenty who was just then climbing into a buckboard beside a grizzled old desert rat whose skin, where it was not covered by a wiry gray beard, resembled nothing so much as an old and wrinkled piece of boot leather. The girl obviously was a stranger to the West, but Chet liked the capable way in which she moved.

Chet's sudden resolution to cross the mountains had been caused by a recollection that his new-found friends, Biggers and Fossum, claimed to be employees of the I X L. It had occurred to him to tell Bud that they were in town, but on second thought he had decided to do the questioning himself.

The two punchers hadn't yet left Curryville, and they had absorbed several whiskies during his absence from the saloon. They greeted him uproariously. He bought a round of drinks, which were consumed at a table, and then ventured an inquiry.

"How long have you boys worked for this here I X L?"

"Oh, 'bout five years," Jack Fossum answered with a maudlin laugh.

"Tell me—what does Charley Harrison do there?" Chet queried.

"Harrison? Ain't nobody o' that name I ever heard tell of over there," Fossum answered. "You, Al?"

"Nope. There's no Harrison in that country I ever heard of," Biggers said. "What made yuh think there was?"

"Well, a man who give that name, an' said he belonged there, was tellin' me how cheap I could buy cows there long before I saw you boys," Chet prevaricated.

"What sort of a lookin' jigger was he?" Fossum asked.

For a moment Chet was stumped. Then he decided to take a chance that Charley Harrison looked like his brother Bud, only larger.

"Well, as I remember," he frowned, "he was jist short o' six feet tall, and he had wavy brown hair, brown eyes, a straight nose an' kinda big mouth, an' a funny little cleft in his chin like a dimple."

"An' did he have a thin scar runnin' from the bridge of his nose to the top of his left eye?" Fossum asked eagerly.

"I believe he did," Chet replied, but he was aware that Al Biggers had given his companion a vicious kick on the shin under the table.

"Yuh musta been mistaken in the name, stranger," Biggers said. "That feller's name was Johnson, not Harrison. He ain't there now."

Chet knew that no more was to be got out of the men, but he had heard enough to know that there was something queer at the I X L ranch, toward which Bud Harrison and his sister were headed. It was none of his business, he knew; and he had made it a lifelong practice to let other people's affairs alone with great diligence. Nevertheless, he didn't like the idea of a girl and a mere boy going alone and unprotected intô a known outlaw country, and he had a reasonable excuse for taking the same trail through the mountains.

"I think I'll just act on that tip you boys gave me," he said softly. "Reckon, I'll start for that Highriver country first thing in the mornin'."

"Yuh'll never regret it, stranger," Al Biggers said fervently. Chet could see the gleam of satisfaction in their eyes. They were too drunk to conceal their animation; yet not drunk enough to overlook any bets.

"I gotta go to Bishop Carey's place tonight, so I may not see you boys again," he remarked.

"Oh, yuh'll see us again—be shore o' that." Biggers laughed. "But let's hoist one."

They had a final drink, and Chet took his departure.

On his buying trips Chet always rode his own private horse, a long-legged, raw-boned gray with a blazed face and two "glass" eyes; an animal with an abundance of speed, and capable of covering from fifty to seventy-five miles day after day without undue fatigue. He called the horse Mike.

No sooner was Chet out of town than he altered his course and worked back to the narrow wagon road which led to Penoloa canyon, the route which he had been told to take. It was all open country so far as fences were concerned, and he kept outside of the road. He let Mike out at a spanking trot until he reached the mouth of the canyon. Here the country was covered with brush and small trees.

He drew his mount to a halt as he saw the buckboard containing the Harrisons and their guide winding up the canyon less than a quarter of a mile distant. As they disappeared around a bend he forced his horse deep into a thicket beside the road, and dismounted where the animal was well out of sight; but where Chet himself could keep an eye upon the road.

Within an hour his vigil was rewarded. Al Biggers and Jack Fossum came shacking along at the familiar jog trot of the range. They seemed hilariously happy.

The corners of Chet Kelvin's mouth crinkled in a somewhat grim smile. He bore no particular malice against his erstwhile boon companions of short acquaintance, but they had told him they meant to proceed in the opposite direction, and now they were going back the way they had come. He thought he knew the reason why.

Then, suddenly, his face became more serious. He had remembered the people in the buckboard ahead. If Biggers and Fossum were, as he had reason to believe, members of the notorious gang of Wild Ones, would they not be liable to attempt a robbery of the other party?

When the two riders had passed on out of sight he led Mike out of the brush, mounted, and proceeded slowly up the canyon.

11

TWO

LEDA HARRISON had become somewhat impatient back in Curryville over her brother's delay in reaching the buckboard when they were ready to start. She was pacing nervously back and forth beside the rig when he arrived.

"Bud, don't you realize that we haven't any time to waste?" she scolded. "Nevada says it will be dark now before we reach the place where he wants to camp."

"I was only a minute late," Bud defended. "I was just talking to that cattle buyer. I thought he might have heard something about Charley."

"Had he?" the girl asked eagerly.

"No; but he said he was heading for Highriver, too, and I invited him to camp with us."

"You shouldn't have done that, Bud," the sister reproved. "This country is beginning to frighten me. It makes me more than ever certain that something is wrong with Charley."

"You cain't be too careful who yuh pick up with, miss," the garrulous old guide chirped. "They say the Wild Ones roams these here parts considerable, an' yuh never kin tell who they are, an' when yuh'll meet up with 'em."

"But this man is a stranger in the country. He couldn't belong to the Wild Ones," Bud insisted.

"You can't be sure of anything," Leda declared. "But there's one thing I'm beginning to be afraid of, and that is that these Wild Ones, as they call themselves, have—have murdered Charley, and stolen his ranch." In spite of her efforts to maintain her self-control, the girl's voice broke. "Otherwise we'd have heard something about him by this time."

"Aw, Charley's all right—he's just been too busy to write," Bud maintained.

Nevada began to whistle to himself in a way which expressed skepticism plainer than words. He had already told the Harrisons that he believed they were upon a wild-goose chase.

"Will you please get started?" Leda urged, half angrily.

"Oh, shore—jest waitin' fer you-all tuh git located," Nevada said cheerfully.

They all three had to squeeze into the one seat of the buckboard, for the long, narrow back of the vehicle was piled high with their camp impedimenta. Leda had chosen to buy their own outfit in preference to depending upon getting meals and lodging in the few remote villages and towns along their way. She had been told that few of them boasted a hotel.

The saving of money also was an important item now. Back in New York state the Harrison family had been an old and respected one. Never extremely wealthy, they had yet managed until recently to escape any privations due to poverty.

Then, just five months ago, Mrs. Harrison had died, following her husband to the grave within two months. Every effort had been made to locate the oldest son, who had gone West five years before, but without avail. Shortly after the funeral the family lawyer had notified Leda that her father had suffered financial reverses, and that even the house and furniture would have to be sold. When the estate was settled less than a thousand dollars remained.

It was then that Leda and Bud had determined to find Charley. Their gay, handsome brother had been home several times after he had gone to the West. He had had plenty of money, and boasted loudly of his big ranch. Young, impressionable Bud had fairly worshiped this big, swashbuckling brother. Leda, too, had thought him wonderful; but lately she recalled that her parents had retired from society about the time Charley had first left New York. And they had not seemed greatly impressed by Charley's display of wealth. Despite their own reverses they had refused to accept the money he had offered them. But this Leda had attributed to their stubborn pride. She believed that their lives had been shortened because of financial worries.

The girl was of a practical mind. Charley had money, and if he was dead she knew that she and Bud were his heirs, unless he had married. It was Charley she wanted to find, but if something had happened she intended to see what had become of his money. She didn't care so much for herself, but Bud was entitled to an education and she meant to see that he got it.

She had been both amazed and awed by the size of the country into which she had landed. She was just now beginning to get her bearings. It had been different with Bud. He had liked the country from the first. The more lonely it was the more he gloried in it.

"The only thing wrong with this outfit," he asserted, as he settled himself on the left side of the seat, "is that I wish I had a saddle horse. When we get to Charley's ranch you bet I'm going to have me a horse and saddle."

"We don't know what we'll get when we reach Charley's ranch," Leda reminded.

"An' you said a mouthful then," Nevada concurred.

As the buckboard started up Penoloa canyon the girl was conscious that they were at last beginning the final leg of

13

their journey. In four more days, Nevada had told her, they would reach the town of Highriver, and learn the truth about the I X L ranch.

They had got well into the canyon, and the buckboard was worming its bumpy way beneath the towering red cliffs which walled the canyon when they were overtaken by two horsemen. Leda, seated in the middle, felt their guide stiffen, and there was a quaver in his voice as he spoke to the team of ponies.

The riders parted, and passed one on each side of the buckboard. They were young, hard-bitten fellows, dressed in the usual trappings of rangeland; wide-brimmed, flat-topped hats; silk neckerchiefs, tied loosely at their throats; blue shirts and overalls, the latter pretty much covered by their leather, batwing chaps. Their feet were encased in the high-heeled boots with which Leda was beginning to be familiar. Charley Harrison had brought much the same kind of regalia home with him on the occasion of his last visit, and as soon as they reached the West Bud had insisted upon getting a similar outfit.

In addition to this, each rider wore a filled cartridge belt slung loosely about his waist, and a heavy Colt's .45 swung low at his right thigh in an open-topped holster. Each man carried a carbine under the fender leather of his saddle.

The riders were grinning, but they sized up the outfit with eyes that missed nothing. Leda felt herself coloring under their scrutiny.

"What yuh blushin' about, sister?" one of them jibed good-naturedly. "You ain't got nothin' you need tuh be ashamed of."

"Aw, come on, Jack," the other said angrily, "we've gotta git tuh Hopkins' ranch 'fore dark."

"Naw, wait a minute," Jack Fossum said drunkenly. "Mebbe little sister here wants a drink." He drew a pint flask out of his chaps pocket and airily extended it toward the girl.

"Thank you, I don't drink," Leda refused icily.

"No? Don't drink? Why, yuh don't know what yo're missin'. How 'bout you, old badger?"

"Th-th-thanks. I n-never refuse go-good whisky," Nevada said, and taking the proffered bottle he let the fiery liquid run down his throat in a gurgling stream. The contents had decreased perceptibly when he handed it back.

"Aw, come on, Jack," Al Biggers rasped.

"Shore—just as soon's I drink toas' to the purtiest dang gal ever seen in Utah. Here's to yuh, miss. The next best thing to the lips of a good-lookin' girl is the lip of a bottle."

With the same motion which withdrew the bottle from his mouth he flung it against the hub of the buckboard, and emitted a yell which mingled discordantly with the crash of glass, and rolled the spurs to his mount. He passed his companion, who also hooked in his spurs, and they galloped out of sight.

"I thought you told me you didn't drink," Leda accused the guide.

"I think too much o' my health not tuh drink when I'm asked to by the Wild Ones," Nevada replied.

"You mean you think those men are—are outlaws?"

"I'll bet seven dollars an' a half they are," Nevada stated positively.

"Then why didn't they hold us up?" Bud demanded.

"They ain't fools, but we ain't outa the woods yit," Nevada said gloomily. "I wish tuh the Lord there was some cut-off we could take."

"You mean you're afraid those men will come back and rob us?" Leda demanded. "They wouldn't dare. We would identify them."

"I wouldn't be too shore about that," Nevada demurred. "If yuh got any val'ables yuh'd better keep 'em well hid. Where'd yuh keep yore money anyway?"

"In—in here," Leda replied with a blush, as she touched the bodice of her dress. "They—they wouldn't dare."

"I wouldn't bank on that either," the guide said pessimistically.

It would soon be dark, and Nevada constantly urged his ponies so as to reach a small, grassy park where he meant to camp. Leda could not restrain the feeling of acute uneasiness which crept over her. Suppose those men were outlaws, and should force her to hand over the money? It was all that she and Bud had in the world. If they couldn't find Charley they would be at the mercy of this forbidding land. The very thought caused her a shudder.

"Gettin' cold, miss?" Nevada queried. "We'll soon be there. Gid-ap, Snip. Hustle along thar, Coley."

The little park was reached just as twilight was settling down over the canyon. Already the sides of the canyon walls resembled the frowning fronts of monster citadels. The park itself was a couple of acres of open grass where a tiny stream cataracted down a precipitous side-canyon.

Nevada proved himself an expert camp attendant, whatever his other shortcomings. He leaped to the ground and had the team unhitched and unharnessed almost before Bud and Leda could get the cramp out of their limbs. Five minutes later he had a cheerful fire burning, and the Easterners crouched around it gratefully. The chill of the mountains had descended as soon as the sun was out of sight.

The tents were quickly set up, and almost before they knew it Nevada had a savory supper of beefsteak, potatoes, and coffee cooking on the coals. But before they were ready to eat darkness had settled about them until there was nothing but a black void between the ring of firelight and the ghostly luminosity of the star-bathed crags.

"Don't be fretted, miss, if yuh hear noises ye ain't used to in the town where ye was raised," Nevada attempted to be reassuring when he saw Leda start at some strange cry from far above them. Then he went on practically to frustrate his own purpose.

"This here country is plumb lousy with b'ars an' mountain lions which'll prob'ly come sniffin' 'round the camp atter we git tuh bed, but they won't hurt nothin' if ye jest lay still."

"Oh!" the girl gasped.

"Gee!" Bud ejaculated.

"Don't worry. I got my old forty-five-seventy an' I'll have 'er right handy tuh my hand," Nevada boasted.

From just behind sounded a chuckle. All three became motionless.

"Hold the pose, everybody," a jeering voice commanded. "Don't reach for that forty-five-seventy now because this ain't no b'ar. It's a stick-up."

THREE

CHET KELVIN had decided not to force his company upon the people in the buckboard until he knew that he would be welcomed. True, he had Bud's invitation, but Bud was only a boy. His sister might resent strangers coming to their camp.

As a rule the cattle buyer traveled without camping equipment, knowing there were few ranches, no matter how remote, which wouldn't welcome a wayfarer. When necessary he hired a pack outfit. On this occasion there had seemed no need for one. Biggers and Fossum had assured him that there were scattered ranches all along the way. They had told him that he could make it from Curryville to Hopkins' ranch in half a day.

He suspected that this ranch was the destination of the two young outlaws themselves, and that it was their intention to hold him up some time the next forenoon. He was curious to see if he had guessed rightly, so he had no intention of ramming into Hopkins' ranch ahead of schedule. But he did wonder if the gay young riders wouldn't try to hold up the buckboard.

He had purposely dallied along behind the buckboard until it grew dark, and then he had easily passed their camp in the shadows of the cliff. Had they had a dog he might have been discovered, but they hadn't, and he could distinctly see them limned against the blackness beyond the fire.

A half mile above the park he had paused. He always carried the makings of a couple of meals rolled up in the blankets on the back of his saddle for emergencies, but he had eaten late, and he merely unsaddled, staked his horse out of sight of the road, and unrolled his blankets.

He didn't go to bed. For a long time he sat with a blanket around his shoulders, and smoked; being careful to see that the glow from his cigaret was never visible from the road.

At last he caught a sound which a city man would never have been able to distinguish—the faint creaking of saddle leather from up the canyon. Instantly he rose, put out his cigaret, and walked over to his horse. With his hand over Mike's nostrils he waited for the two horsemen to pass; then, silently as any Indian, he followed them.

The men were riding slowly, and he almost blundered upon them when they suddenly stopped. They continued on foot. From where they left their horses the glow of the camp-fire below could be plainly seen. Despite the darkness Chet recognized the two horses as the ones Biggers and Fossum had been riding. These bad boys of the range were certainly up to mischief.

He knew that they had delayed long enough to draw their bandannas over their faces, and now he proceeded to do the same thing. Then, gun in hand, he moved slowly toward the fire.

He wasn't close enough to hear what was said, but he had a fine view of the little pantomime that was enacted beside the fire. He saw the three victims suddenly grow rigid, and then a single masked man advanced like a moving silhouette. He dared not get too close. To interfere with the hold-up there would be too dangerous to the people of the buckboard; so he had to be where he could beat the outlaws back to their horses.

He could dimly make out one outlaw keeping among the shadows while his companion did the robbing. First, he saw old Nevada rise and submit to search, and then back up against the fire. Then Bud was frisked by the same outlaw, and made to join Nevada. Chet was breathing hard when he saw the outlaw approach the girl and apparently order her to stand up.

17

Leda Harrison got up, but her every movement registered defiance. The outlaw was holding out his hand, but the girl was putting nothing into it.

They seemed to be having a spirited argument. The girl was pointing toward a satchel, which the outlaw finally investigated but apparently found little to his liking.

Then, suddenly, the girl made a desperate lunge to get in front of her brother, but the outlaw caught her arm and swung her back. For a moment the fellow held her close, and Chet hurriedly moved a rod closer. He stopped as he clearly heard the girl's agitated voice.

"Let me go! If you touch my brother I'll kill you."

Chet couldn't hear what the outlaws were saying, but he didn't need to hear to know what it was all about. The second man was threatening to harm the boy unless the girl surrendered what they wanted. Chet knew that it was probably all bluff, and that if the girl held out they would go away. But the girl didn't know that.

There was some more wrangling, and suddenly a pencil of yellow flame leaped out of the darkness from the unseen outlaw's gun. At the sound of the shot Bud Harrison staggered and almost fell. He was caught by Nevada. The shot had blasted the heel off one of Bud's new boots.

"Don't, don't shoot again," the girl screamed wildly. "I'll give you all I've got."

"Don't yuh do it, sis. Don't yuh let 'em have it," Bud cried out, but the girl had turned her back to the two outlaws, and Chet could see her reaching down into the front of her dress A moment later she turned back and handed something to the outlaw.

The fellow hurriedly thumbed the packet he had received, and then thrust it carelessly into his inside pocket. He seemed in no hurry to depart. The girl had backed toward the buckboard, while the fellow seemed to be joking her about something. Then, apparently, his companion interfered and he desisted. But he moved over to where Nevada's rifle was lying, took the weapon by the barrel and flung it far down the canyon. It struck with a crash against a rock.

Chet hastily moved back to where the outlaws' horses stood, and as they came back they were plainly visible against the firelight in the background. They were twenty feet distant when he spoke.

"Git 'em up, hombres, an' raise 'em fast," he ordered.

The outlaws stopped as if they had butted into a stone wall. For an instant there was the expected interval of hesitation while they debated whether to obey the startling command, or try to shoot it out. Chet had little fear as to what they

18

would do. Given an instant to think they would know better than to try gunplay when they were already covered. And despite what he had just seen Chet didn't figure the two to be real killers. They might kill if crowded, but they were more given to dare-deviltry than viciousness—or so he had sized them up that afternoon.

After that momentary hesitation their hands went up.

"That's fine, boys," Chet approved. "I don't want a thing except what you took from those people there, but I can't have you gummin' up my game like that."

"Who the hell are you?" Al Biggers growled.

"Just call me Nemesis," Chet grinned. "Now just unbuckle your gun belts an' let 'em drop. That's the boy. Now step away from 'em. Fine. Now I'm gonna toss my hat on the ground, an' I want yuh tuh put everything yuh got from those people in it. Don't try holdin' anything back, because I was watchin' every move yuh made, an' I know what yuh got."

"All right, Mr. Knee Measles, you got the high card, but yuh can't buck the Wild Ones an' git away with it," Al Biggers said.

Chet suspected that it was a teaser to find out if he was himself a member of the gang who didn't know who they were.

"Wild Ones, me eye," he jeered. "Stacked against real bad-men you lads would look like Sunday-school boys."

"Mebbe you wouldn't be so hard yoreself, hombre, if yuh was stacked up against Kirk Holliday an' Blackie Payne," the man snarled. He had named the two chief leaders of the Wild Ones.

"Come on, drop that stuff in the hat," Chet ordered curtly. "I'm conductin' this meetin', an' I aim tuh git a full collection."

The last article to be dropped was the packet which the girl had taken from the bosom of her dress, and Al Biggers had to be told the second time to let it go.

"All right, boys," Chet remarked cheerfully. "Back away now while I git the hat. Then stand where you are and count a hundred before you move. Don't count too fast either if you don't want tuh stop a bullet."

Hat in hand Chet withdrew silently into the shadows and waited. The two young outlaws had ample time to count several hundred before they moved. Then they picked up their weapons, mounted their horses, and rode away into the night. Chet grinned. He had but one worry concerning them; that was that they might hear his horse on their way back.

A more immediate worry was how to return the loot to those it belonged to. It would have been easy to walk boldly in and pass the money over, but he had a natural aversion to heroics. Besides, he had other plans with which such a procedure would interfere.

Then it occurred to him that he didn't need to show himself to return the money. Right now Nevada was piling dry wood on the fire, and wavering lights were dancing far across the little park.

"Hello!" he shouted presently.

Immediately the three at the fire became rigid. Chet couldn't blame them for being nervous.

"Who—who—who is there?" Nevada quavered. His voice sounded so much like the hooting of an owl that Chet laughed.

"I'm a friend," Chet replied. "Listen: Those bandits lost the money they took from you. If you'll come over here you'll find it on the ground right where I am now."

He wasn't answered at once. The three around the fire counseled together. Nevada apparently suspected a trick, but Bud seized a flaming torch and came forward. His sister followed.

Chet hastily dumped the contents of his hat on the ground and withdrew to where he could watch in safety. By the light from Bud's torch he saw them find the money and pick it up. Their pleasure and relief was a joy to watch.

"Hey, won't yuh come over to the camp? We want to thank you for giving our money back," Bud called.

Chet made no answer. He saw them vainly trying to pierce the darkness, and he had to throw himself flat to escape detection when the boy suddenly and unexpectedly extinguished the torch. They returned to the camp at last, and Kelvin made his way back to his horse.

Mike was grazing undisturbed, and Chet rolled peacefully into his blankets.

The next morning Chet was awakened by the rattling of wheels. It was only a little past daybreak, but the Harrison party was already on the move—anxious to get out of Penoloa canyon before other misadventures befell them. Sitting up in his blankets he watched them through a screen of bushes as they passed. They seemed happy. He smiled. This being a sort of modern Robin Hood made a man feel good.

He could dismiss them from his mind for the present. His concern now was with the two young outlaws he had held up. He wondered if they would attempt to hold him up as they had surely planned, or if their experience of the night before had soured them on hold-ups for the time being.

He built a fire and leisurely cooked breakfast. Mike had

20

eaten all he wanted and was resting on three legs while his eyes curiously followed the movements of his master.

At last Chet saddled the horse, tied the blanket-roll firmly in place, and rode up the canyon. He rode with seeming carelessness, and he had taken off his gun belt and hooked it over the saddle horn as men frequently do on long rides to avoid the drag at their waists. Yet he was alert, and his keen eyes missed no movement in the brush.

He hadn't decided what he would do if he were held up. He had a hundred and fifty dollars expense money on him, but he didn't propose to get himself killed trying to save it. The only thing that really worried him was that they might take his horse. If they didn't leave him afoot he was confident that he could recover his other property eventually, Wild Ones or no Wild Ones.

His speculations were wasted. Shortly before noon he emerged from the narrow canyon onto a sort of plateau, broken by rolling hills and long, shallow ravines. If the outlaws had been going to hold him up they would have done so in the canyon.

A mile to his right he saw a log cabin, and a fenced pasture. This he judged to be Hopkins' ranch. He was convinced that it was a rendezvous for the Wild Ones—in fact, Kirk Holliday's gang had many such places scattered throughout the range country. It was nearly dinner time, and without the least hesitation he headed for the cabin.

As he rode up he saw four saddled horses tied close to the cabin, and an equal number of men were outside in the shade. Another man was inside cooking dinner. And two of those men were Al Biggers and Jack Fossum. The latter was grinning up at Chet like a Cheshire cat. Biggers' eyes glimmered with suspicion.

Before he spoke Chet cast a swift glance at the other two men. One was small, dark and wiry; so very dark, in fact, that Chet suspected the man of having Indian or Mexican blood. The other was a blond young giant, with a pleasant face, but with baby blue eyes which were anything but innocent. Chet knew instinctively that those eyes were shrewd in the reading of faces, and he suspected that a flinty hardness lay behind their bland good-nature.

Members of the Wild Ones, Chet catalogued them instantly. But he would have been utterly amazed had he known that the blond giant was none other than Kirk Holliday, the leader of the Wild Ones, and that the dark-skinned fellow was Blackie Payne, his chief lieutenant—a man who would shoot to kill upon the slightest provocation, and who had been known to shoot a man for asking if he was an Indian.

21

"Well, well, Mr. Kelvin," Jack Fossum greeted genially. "We been waitin' for yuh."

FOUR

CHET KELVIN would have been less than human had the present situation created no nervousness. His thoughts clicked with lightning speed, and he wondered if the hold-up he had expected back in the canyon was to come off now, or if, perhaps, the men knew that it was he who had turned the tables the night before, and were about to exact some more sinister vengeance. But he knew that it would do no good to betray either fear or too much surprise.

"Why, hello, hombres," he greeted easily. "This is a surprise to see you here. I thought yuh was headed for Pipe Springs."

Jack Fossum got lazily to his feet and stretched.

"Git down, pardner, git down," he invited. "Our good friend Hopkins'll have dinner ready in a jiff. I'll tell him tuh lay another plate."

"That'll be fine," Chet said, as he threw his left leg over the saddle horn and dropped to the ground. "It was thinkin' about dinner which headed me over here in the first place. Wonder if I can git a feed of grain for my horse, or else turn him somewhere?"

"I'll see," Fossum said, and disappeared inside the cabin.

Kelvin was acutely aware that his two erstwhile drinking companions had failed to account for their change of plan. It wasn't reassuring.

The blond giant looked up indolently. "How far yuh made today?" he queried.

"Can't just say," Chet replied just as casually. "Stayed all night with a Mormon bishop name of Carey."

"Yeah, I know him," the blond man nodded. "In fact, I figger on stayin' there m'self tonight." He looked up quickly, but if he had expected to discover signs of confusion on the cattle buyer's face he was disappointed.

"That hawse o' yore's don't look like he'd come that far this mawnin'," spoke up the little dark man.

"I left before daylight, an' my horse has got a runnin' walk that don't sweat nor tire him," Chet replied a bit curtly.

It was the blond man who answered. "I see," he nodded. "Does look like a right good horse. Orta have speed. I bet you could clean up some good money with him if you was tuh

22

run into the Wild Ones. Kirk Holliday thinks he knows horses, an' they say yuh kin always git a trade with him."

"That so? Mebbe I'll look Mr. Holliday up—after I git my business done," Chet said evenly.

"That reminds me—I been waitin' here just tuh talk business with you. What the hell's the matter with you, Al—why don't yuh introduce us tuh the stranger?"

Chet felt that something was coming off, and whatever it was he was certain the men intended for him to get the worst of it. But he continued to smile, and hoped that it wasn't too mechanical.

"Oh, excuse me," Biggers mumbled. "Kelvin, I wantcha tuh meet my friend Hank Stevens, o' Stag-tail butte."

The blond giant leaped gracefully to his feet, and shook hands cordially. He had a firm, hearty handshake. "Plumb glad tuh know yuh," he said warmly. "Plumb."

"An' I'm glad tuh meet you," Chet responded.

"An' this is 'Happy' Mack, Mr. Kelvin," Biggers introduced the little dark man.

Mack didn't rise. He had been sitting with his knees cocked up, rolling a cigaret. "How," he grinned, and offered the makings.

"Thanks," Chet drawled.

Jack Fossum came out of a lean-to at one end of the cabin with a nose-bag two-thirds full of oats. Out of the corner of his eye Chet noticed that the lean-to was full of sacked grain.

"Here yuh are, Chet, old boy. Slip this on that glass-eyed giraffe, an' dinner is all ready," Fossum said cheerfully.

The Mike horse had moved a few yards away to a water trough made out of half a whisky barrel, where he was drinking noisily through the bit. Fossum walked over to the trough with Chet.

"Did yuh give it back?" he queried in a half whisper.

"Huh?" Chet blurted. Then he grinned as the young outlaw gave him a wink. He realized that there was no use to make a denial. Fossum, at least, knew that he was the man who had, as it were, plundered the Philistines.

"Naturally," he said. "If I'd been goin' tuh keep anything I'd have took everything but yore underwear."

"That's what I thought," Fossum said. "Biggers thinks it was you, but he ain't sure. Take a tip from me, brother, an' hit the back trail."

The nose-bag was fastened on and they had to turn back. Chet was more puzzled than ever.

"Jack," he said loud enough for the others to hear, "you ain't told me yet how yuh happened tuh change yore mind about goin' tuh Pipe Springs."

23

"Oh, that," Fossum said. "We found out there was a letter in the Curryville post office from our boss tellin' us he'd changed his mind, an' orderin' us tuh come back. We left town right after you did a little while. In fact we got here just at dark, an' have been here ever since, eh, Mark?"

The lantern-jawed nester had come out to announce dinner, and he nodded a quick affirmation. "Yep, the boys have been right here. I'm allus glad tuh have comp'ny."

"I see," Chet murmured. And he did see a carefully arranged alibi if the men should be accused of robbing the Harrisons. What he couldn't understand was young Fossum's attitude.

"We'd have been a long way on our road if we hadn't met Hank an' Happy here," Fossum chattered. "When we found out Hank was tryin' tuh sell his cattle we remembered about you, an' so we agreed tuh wait here with 'em till yuh come along."

"So you have some cattle tuh sell?" Chet remarked to the man who called himself Stevens.

"Yeah, I have got a few," the big blond man acknowledged, his baby-blue eyes meeting Chet's with a cold and scrutinizing stare. The cattle buyer knew then that his first impression about the hardness of those eyes had been correct. Hank Stevens was a man who meant to have the best of a bargain.

"Well," Chet said cheerfully, as they all seated themselves around the bare board table, which, though innocent of any vestige of covering, was laden with food both plentiful and palatable, "that's my business. I'll be glad to look yore stuff over."

For just an instant he caught a flicker of cynical amusement in Jack Fossum's eyes. This, then, was what he had been warned to beware of.

"That suits me fine," Stevens said. "We ain't got no market up around Stag-tail. If I drive out tuh these Mormon towns they skin me, an' I don't know nothin' about the markets up north."

"I see," Chet murmured vaguely. Unless this young fellow's looks deceived him mightily he would be hard to "skin." Certainly the phlegmatic Mormons Chet had met, such as Bishop Carey, were not in the same class with this falsely humble young cattleman.

Chet was picking thoughts out of the air like a bird catching bugs, but none of them were satisfactory. He believed thoroughly that he had got mixed up with a portion of the far-famed Wild Ones. He didn't believe that young Hank Stevens had any more ranch than a horse has horns, but he couldn't

24

understand their game. If robbery only was their object, why didn't they get it over with?

"I can't git my stuff gathered under about two weeks," Stevens remarked. "But if you're goin' down tuh buy some stuff at the I X L an' trail it north across the Castle mountains I'll have my herd ready tuh throw into yours about a hundred miles north of there if we kin make a deal."

"That might be satisfactory," Chet said noncommittally. He had decided to play the cards as they fell, and he was now the astute but deliberate buyer of cattle. "What kind of stuff have you got, an' what figure do you hold 'em at?"

For the next thirty minutes he and Stevens tested each other, haggling about the price of cattle as though they had been about to consummate a real deal. Chet found out that Stevens really knew what cattle were worth, and what he didn't know his supposed foreman, Happy Mack, did. They admitted that their cattle were small and wild, and they insisted that Chet buy them as they came, from old cows to calves. But the price Stevens agreed to accept was not unreasonable.

"Well, mebbe we can do business," Chet said finally. "I'll go down to this I X L an' see what I can do there first."

"But we can't afford tuh round up everything unless we know we can make a deal," Stevens protested.

"You'll just have to take a chance on that," Chet retorted good-naturedly. "If the stuff is as good as you claim and I can get enough to make up my trail herd, I'll buy. Of course I'll expect you to produce full proof of ownership."

"Yeah, sure," Stevens said quickly. "An' I'll expect you to pay cash on the dot."

It was almost too obvious. With the lure of a profitable deal they hoped to inveigle him into carrying a big sum of money out on the range where he could be robbed.

"I never carry much money about with me, but we can arrange that," he said coldly.

Except for just one thing Kelvin would have abandoned the whole project at the first opportunity, as Jack Fossum had advised. But that one thing had to do with the young Harrisons. They were on their way to the I X L ranch under the mistaken impression that it belonged to their brother. For all Chet knew it did belong to Charley Harrison, and the man might have been murdered or otherwise foully dealt with. But it was assuredly under outlaw control now, and Leda Harrison and her kid brother were rushing blindly into the utmost danger.

He wasn't called upon to act as their guardian, but, strangely enough, since he had interceded to save them from being the victims of robbery, he felt more or less responsible for

25

them. So, after arriving at a tentative understanding with Hank Stevens, he mounted his horse and started for the I X L ranch in company with Biggers and Fossum.

Late that evening they rode into a little range settlement known as Boxtown. As they turned into a ranch house, where his companions said they would be able to put up, they passed within two rods of where the Harrisons and their guide were camped beside a small irrigating ditch.

Both Chet and Jack Fossum lifted their hats and spoke, but they received no acknowledgment.

FIVE

SOMEHOW Chet felt the humiliation of an unnecessary rebuff; even though his sense of justice told him that the Harrisons couldn't be blamed for not speaking. The girl had never spoken to him, but he was sure that she knew who he was. He believed Bud would have hailed him had his sister not told him not to.

They had been held up and robbed, and undoubtedly they suspected Biggers and Fossum regardless of the masks the men had worn. Now seeing him in their company they naturally placed him in the same category.

It was his own fault, he admitted. He had had an opportunity to make himself known when he gave them back their property, but he hadn't done it. Now he would have a hard time making them believe he had been their benefactor.

"Gosh, they act like they don't know us," Jack Fossum grinned.

"That's the trouble—they know you too well," Chet retorted, before he had time to consider the effect.

Instantly Al Biggers gave him a quick, malignant glance.

"I reckon a gal out here like this can't figger she'll git anything that she ain't got comin'," the fellow growled, and then added an obscene comment.

Chet paled with anger, and he involuntarily turned his horse toward the outlaw. Biggers had his hand upon his gun, and his eyes glared hatred. Chet hesitated. He was determined not to let the insult to the girl pass unrebuked, but he was reluctant to start anything within sight and hearing of the Harrison camp. But before either man could disclose his intentions Jack Fossum intervened.

"Cut that, Al," he said crisply. "That's a decent girl, an' there's no call for you makin' a crack like that. Git me?" The smaller outlaw's voice fairly bristled.

"The hell yuh bawl out," Biggers snarled, turning his attention to his partner. "Who was gittin' gay with her yesterday?"

"I was drunk," Fossum said. "But I didn't make no rotten remark to or about her. I know a thoroughbred when I see one."

"Oh, yeah?" Biggers sneered.

Chet wisely dropped back a pace. So long as Fossum had taken it up first he saw no reason to interfere.

"Yeah," Fossum shot back. "An' if you ever make a crack like that again I'll climb yuh like a tree. An' git yore hand off'n that gun."

"Oh, all right; it ain't wuth havin' a row about," Biggers growled.

"An' what Jack says goes for me," Chet said. "I've never spoke to that girl in my life, but if I've got any say about it she can travel as safely here as she could in her own dooryard."

"I've noticed that you've kinda appointed yoreself her guardian," Biggers said.

"I don't have tuh do that—she don't need a guardian," Chet retorted.

He could see that Jack Fossum was trying to signal his companion, and he guessed that Fossum's interference had been dictated solely by a desire to prevent a quarrel which might result in the loss of profits the Wild Ones hoped to gain.

"Well, here we are," Fossum said cheerfully. "Let's quit chewin' the fat an' see about supper."

They were told to turn their horses into a pasture, and invited to sleep in the haymow of a large barn. The rancher refused to take pay for their meals.

At supper Chet noticed that in spite of all the hospitality displayed the rancher and his family were afraid of them. He was later to learn that it was this fear on the part of the people in the remote localities which made the depredations of the Wild Ones possible. They dared not inform on the Wild Ones or refuse to aid them when necessary. In return, Kirk Holliday and his men offered them a certain immunity from their merciless exploitation.

Notwithstanding the attitude of the Harrisons, Chet was determined to have a talk with them before he left Boxtown. He knew it might be his last opportunity, for he and his companions would travel much faster than the buckboard possibly could. But the opportunity did not present itself until the next morning.

Chet was the first one out of the loft after they heard the rancher come out to milk his cows. There was a small pony in the stable and he promptly borrowed it to run in their horses. He mounted the animal bareback, and had just found the horses at the lower end of the pasture when he saw Bud Harrison coming after their team on foot. It had been turned into the same pasture.

Immediately Chet cut the team of ponies in with his own horses and drove them toward the boy. He helped Bud catch the one which Nevada called Coley, and when the boy had got on the horse Chet proceeded to help him drive the entire band toward the Harrison camp.

"Well, how have you liked the trip this far, Bud?" he asked.

The boy gazed at him uncertainly. He had not as yet spoken.

"It's been exciting at any rate," he replied finally.

"Oh, is that so?" Chet asked innocently.

"When did you leave Curryville?" Bud asked bluntly.

Chet hesitated, but he found it impossible to lie to the boy.,

"Not long after you did," he admitted.

"Did you pass our camp last night?"

"Yes, I did."

"Why didn't you stop? I invited you to camp with us."

"Well, since I had never met yore sister I didn't figger it would be just proper for me tuh come bustin' in on yuh," Chet said.

"Look here, Mr. Kelvin," the boy burst out, "we were stuck up last night, and my sister had to turn over all our money to a couple of thugs."

"Yuh don't say!" Chet exclaimed.

"We think we know who they were," the boy went on. "We think they were the two fellows you were with last night."

"I wouldn't put it a-past 'em," Chet nodded.

"But somebody held them up and made 'em give our stuff back," Bud volunteered. "He didn't show himself, but we surely owe him a lot. I don't know what we'd have done if we hadn't got our money back."

"Well, I'm certainly glad yuh had such good luck," Chet said warmly.

"Know what my sister thinks? She thinks all three of them fellows are members of those Wild Ones we've heard so much about. She thinks that the one that made 'em give the money back thought it was too dirty a trick to rob us, and so he made his pals give it back. Yuh know they claim Kirk Holliday never robs poor people."

The boy leaned far over his pony's withers, but he was watching the cattle buyer narrowly.

"And maybe she's wrong," Chet contended quietly. "Maybe those two were just drunk enough to think it would be a good

28

joke to scare you a little, an' intended tuh give it back themselves in a little while."

The boy was frankly astonished.

"You think that was how it was?" he asked eagerly. "They was drunk when they passed us. But Nevada says he's dead sure they're all three Wild Ones."

"I think that's how it was," Chet said. "But I think mebbe I've kinda got some track of yore brother. That's why I wanted tuh talk with you this mornin'."

"You have? You know where Charley is? Gee, that's great!"

"Not so fast," Chet remonstrated. "I've only got the slimmest kind of a clue. It may not be anything at all. Tell me, do you remember if your brother had a thin scar from the top of his nose over above his left eye?"

"Yes, he did," the boy said eagerly. "I remember about him having it the last time he came home. When we asked him how he got it he laughed and said he'd got it in a fight with one of Kirk Holliday's Wild Ones."

"Then you'd heard about the Wild Ones before you came out here?"

"Oh, yes. We'd read about 'em in the papers, and then Charley told us a lot more about their ways. But what else have you found out about Charley?" Bud demanded impatiently.

"Not a thing," Chet answered.

They had now reached a point where he must turn off toward the corral, or else continue on to the Harrison camp. He was relieved when Bud insisted that he ride on to their camp.

For some strange reason Chet found himself trembling at the prospect of talking with Leda Harrison. He wasn't usually nervous in the presence of girls, for all that he seldom sought their society. The cold, impersonal look the girl gave him didn't ease his self-consciousness to any extent.

"Say, sis, Mr. Kelvin here knows something about Charley," Bud announced excitedly.

Leda looked up quickly, and her eyes sought the cattle buyer's face with an unvoiced hope. Her expression quickly changed to one of suspicion.

"You—you have met my brother?" she asked in a low voice.

"I'm sorry to say I never have," Chet said. "I'm a stranger in this country, like yourself. But after Bud told me about him, I made some inquiries from the two men I'm traveling with, after I found out they worked on this I X L outfit you say your brother owned."

Leda Harrison's reticence disappeared before her intense desire to get information.

"Those men work for the I X L, you say? And they know my brother?" she cried.

"They claim to work for the I X L. Whether they do or not I can't say, but they deny all knowledge of your brother."

"But the scar?" Bud put in.

"One of them mentioned that when I was makin' my inquiries, but the other man said the fellow who had such a scar was named Johnson," Chet was compelled to admit.

"Then—then you don't know anything about my brother after all," the girl said dismally.

"But if those fellows work on the I X L they must have known Charley," Bud argued.

"Yes," the girl said. "They must know what has happened to him. If—if—he has been done away with they must have had a hand in it. They are outlaws, I'm sure. I'm certain that the man who took our money last night was the fellow who offered me a drink from his whisky bottle."

"And the other cuss was the one who shot the heel off my boot," Bud added.

The boy lifted a brand-new boot and gazed ruefully at the place where the long, forward-jutting heel had been.

"There does seem to be something queer about the business," Chet admitted. "They say the I X L belongs to a man by the name of Adam Broome—a man well past sixty. Don't you think it would be well if you had somebody else investigate for you, before you went down there?"

All the girl's latent suspicion flared anew.

"Outlaws or not, I mean to find out for myself what happened to my brother," she declared.

"Hey, look out!" Chet yelled, pointing toward the fire. A pan of bacon on the coals had suddenly caught fire. Nevada was busy at the buckboard. Leda turned, and grasped the handle of the skillet in her bare hand. The handle was hot and she juggled it wildly for a minute from one hand to the other. Then, just as she had to let it go, a calloused paw seized the handle just below her hand and placed the skillet on the ground.

"I'm afraid I was too late tuh save the bacon, but I hope yuh didn't git burned," Chet said.

The girl displayed two soft palms across which wavered several long white welts.

"I—I—guess I'm not much good at this camp-fire cooking," she faltered. "But I'll learn," she added grimly.

"Have yuh got some soda?" Chet demanded, and when Nevada hurriedly produced a package he put some on the girl's painful burns, and urged her to continue the application until the pain was relieved.

"It's better already," she said. "Thank you for helping me."

"Sorry I couldn't do more," Chet said. "And I'd like tuh do something tuh help yuh find yore brother."

"I'm afraid we owe you something already," she said. "Aren't you the man who gave us back our money?"

She was looking straight at him out of honest golden-brown eyes which wouldn't be denied. He couldn't lie to her.

"Yes, I'm the man," he admitted.

"And those other two were the men who held us up?"

"Yes."

The question he had dreaded came as inexorably as doom.

"Then why are you traveling with them?"

He couldn't tell her that it was because he wanted to protect her and her brother, and no other reason would suffice, unless he branded himself as a crook.

"We just happen tuh be travelin' in the same direction," he said weakly. "As for the robbery, it was probably a drunken prank. No doubt they would have given you back yore money later."

"It was no prank," she declared. "And if it was a joke it was just as reprehensible."

"I agree with you," was all Chet could find to say. He had no excuse for reopening the discussion about her brother; no reason for delaying his departure. Leda Harrison knew that his two companions were outlaws, and she knew that he knew it. He had returned her money, but that couldn't condone his evil association in her eyes.

"It'd been a dang poor joke on them fellers if they hadn't busted my rifle." Nevada spoke up. "If they hadn't bent the bar'l around like a letter 's,' I'd uh trailed 'em tuh Kirk Holliday's own bailiwick but what I'd uh got that money back."

"Well, I hope you don't have no more bad luck," Chet mumbled, and remounted his pony. He could see Biggers and Fossum watching him, so he herded the horses on to the corral.

"Why don't yuh invite yore friends along when yuh go callin'?" Al Biggers inquired sourly.

"I don't pay social calls this early in the mornin'," Chet replied evenly. "I was just helpin' the kid ketch his horses."

"Yeah? Took yuh a long time, didn't it?"

"That girl burned her hand. I helped wrap it up."

"What the hell is that outfit doin' in here? Where they headin'?" Biggers demanded.

"To tell the truth," Chet said, looking the man straight in the eye, "they're lookin' for that man Charley Harrison I spoke tuh you about. He's their brother."

31

"The hell he is!" Biggers blurted.

"Are you sure you boys don't remember him?"

"There never was nobody in this country by that name," Biggers asserted flatly.

"Mebbe he went by another name," Chet murmured. "They claim that he owned the I X L."

"Owned the—" Biggers paused abruptly and directed a glance at his companion.

Chet saw Fossum shake his head slightly.

"Somebody," the outlaw said heavily, "has been feedin' 'em taffy. The I X L has belonged tuh old Adam Broome for twenty years."

SIX

CHET KELVIN had nearly two more days in which to study his two companions. That they had once planned to rob him, he knew. That they might attempt to do so again was entirely probable. If anything at all deterred them it was that they now hoped to profit from him in a far larger way if they could prevail upon him to produce a big bundle of cash to pay for the supposititious cattle of their friend "Hank Stevens."

Immediately after leaving Boxtown Chet's suspicions of his companions flamed anew. Before leaving Curryville he had ascertained the best route to the Highriver country, and he knew that his companions had quit that route at Boxtown. To his ventured remonstrance Jack Fossum explained negligently that they were taking a cut-off.

It was a lonely, God-forsaken land through which they now led him. Despite his ability to take care of himself Chet felt an occasional chill shoot up his spine. A man might be murdered out here and his body not be discovered for months or years. And he knew that there were plenty of bandits who would kill a man to get possession of a horse like glass-eyed Mike, to say nothing of the money Chet carried in his pocket. But apparently his companions entertained only the kindliest thoughts.

Jack Fossum, Chet quickly learned, was naturally a happy-go-lucky fellow of generous and kindly impulses. When he wasn't talking he was singing—as gay a young devil as one could find, but reckless as a bull elk in springtime. He could be led into anything that was dangerous, and he would go through with it for the mere joy of adventure.

Al Biggers was a different type. If he was a bit slow-witted and dull, he was also more cool and deliberate than his companion, and his every act was calculated to benefit Al Biggers. After leaving Boxtown, however, he seemed to shed his dislike and suspicion of Chet and became almost amiable. He sang less than his friend Fossum, but he sang better. And that night around a camp-fire Chet joined with them in singing a dozen or so of the old mournful, and frequently unprintable, songs of cowland.

As their last song died away a coyote on a neighboring knoll parodied the refrain in so melancholy a key that they all laughed.

"He's got the music an' all he lacks is the words," Jack laughed. "Let him finish the concert—I'm goin' tuh bed."

The young outlaw picked up his blankets and carried them a considerable distance from the fire—a precaution which Chet didn't fail to notice. All day Chet had been seeking a chance to talk privately with Fossum, and demand an explanation of his warning at Hopkins' ranch, but there had been no opportunity.

For some time Chet and Biggers sat by the fire talking, and then the big outlaw yawned and reached for his blankets. To Chet's satisfaction he carried them directly opposite to the way Fossum had gone.

Chet sat by the fire and smoked for another half hour. Then he wet down the remaining embers and took his blankets over to where Fossum lay.

"Asleep, Jack?" he inquired softly.

"Naw. Just lookin' at the stars," the outlaw replied. "Funny how they git yuh sometimes, ain't it? Stars remind me of people. Some of 'em are cold an' frosty, like Al Biggers there." He paused and laughed softly.

"An' then there are others," he proceeded, "which are kinda mellow an' soft. But there ain't many like that. There's one star I like better'n any o' the others. It—it reminds me o' my mother. She died when I was five."

Obviously the tough young outlaw was in a rare, sentimental mood.

Chet lay down beside the man and gave him a light for his cigaret.

"I like stars," the outlaw confessed, "especially out on a desert like this where yuh can see so many more of 'em than you can most places. An' everything silent."

"Tell me, Jack, where was yuh raised?"

"Wyoming. My dad was—what the hell do you care what my dad was?" he broke off. "I belong tuh the Wild Ones now."

Chet certainly hadn't expected so frank a confession.

"Why?" he asked mildly.

"What difference does it make?" Young Fossum yawned.

33

"None, of course. Yore business is yore own. But I don't quite get you. You an' Al figgered tuh hold me up—"

"An' yuh beat us to it," Fossum chuckled. "Yo're too tough for us—that's why I tried tuh persuade yuh tuh turn back."

"Yo're a darn liar. What was the reason?"

"I'll tell yuh. In the first place, I kinda took a likin' to yuh. Then after yuh turned the tables on us so slick I figgered you'd be a bad man tuh handle. You're gittin' into wild country, brother, an' if my friend over there finds out for shore it was you who stuck us up he's just ornery enough tuh resent it. An' he'll know before long. He's purty shore now. Tuh save trouble I wanted you tuh turn back."

"That's not all the truth, but I reckon I'll have tuh be satisfied," Chet sighed.

"Lots o' fellers among the Wild Ones don't like tuh be called a liar," Fossum said good-humoredly. "But go ahead. I kin stand abuse."

"Jack, I want tuh know the truth about this Charley Harrison."

"I don't know a thing about him," Fossum said curtly.

"Well, then what about the man with the scar over his eye?" Chet persisted.

"That feller's name is Johnson—'Dude' Johnson."

"Where is he now?" Chet asked, perfectly aware that he was treading on dangerous ground.

It was a minute or more before the outlaw replied. "His last address was the state penitentiary," he said crisply.

It was Chet's turn to seek reflection in silence. "Was he— did he belong to the Wild Ones?"

"You'll have tuh ask Kirk Holliday about that," Fossum returned promptly.

There remained only one more avenue of attack, and Chet approached it with considerable diffidence. Already Fossum had gone a long way in friendliness; he might resent an abuse of it by an attempt to pump him concerning the affairs of the crowd with which he was associated.

"About this I X L ranch where you an' Al say you work," he began. "This Harrison girl says her brother Charley claimed to own the I X L ranch. She thinks he may have been killed, and she is goin' tuh try tuh claim the ranch. What do you think about that?"

"I think she's crazy," Fossum answered. "In the first place, there never was any Charley Harrison here. In the second place, old Adam Broome has been on the I X L for twenty years. If you've got any influence with that girl you'll have her git outa here as quick as the Lord'll let her. An' you go along."

With a grunt the outlaw rolled over in his blankets and turned his back to Chet.

From Jack Fossum's manner in the morning one would have supposed he had entirely forgotten that bedtime conversation. He was as garrulous as usual, and as they rode along later in the day he pointed out to Chet the best way to trail out the cattle which he was presumably going to contract for at the I X L.

For twenty-four hours now they hadn't contacted a ranch; they lived from the small amount of supplies they had brought from Boxtown. These had been exhausted at breakfast, so Chet understood that they would make some ranch by dinner time. They assured him that they would reach the I X L by noon the following day.

About ten o'clock that morning they suddenly altered their course and headed toward what looked to Chet to be the blank face of a great table butte. But when they reached it, half an hour later, he saw that what had appeared to be a solid, projecting sandstone cliff had really been severed by a knife-gash rift which led back across one corner of the butte. Once they were in it they could see nothing for nearly a mile except the yellowish, vertical walls of a canyon.

Then presently they came out on the north side of the butte and took a dim trail which led down through a jungle of mountain manzanita. After a mile or so of this the country opened up into a small basin with natural hay meadows fed by a small stream pouring down from the west. Beyond the meadows was a group of buildings.

· For all that there were obvious possibilities for the making of a fine ranch the place was uncared for. Only a small part of the available hay land had been watered, and the buildings had been innocent of repairs for many a hard winter. A small stack of hay had been put up that summer from where the water had taken its natural course, and there were signs that a camp had been made beside the creek for some time. But the place seemed deserted now.

They turned their horses to the haystack and Chet followed the two men to the house. They seemed perfectly at home. While Biggers made a fire, Jack Fossum opened an old pit in the back and from it produced an abundance of such groceries as could be kept for a long time without spoiling.

Chet knew that it was a good time to say nothing.

"This place belongs tuh a man we know," Fossum explained presently. "He lives in Highriver, an' just comes out here tuh put up a li'l hay for spring use."

"I see," Chet said. It was plausible enough, except that it seemed strange the man would have camped out by the creek,

35

and left supplies at the house after the need for them had passed. He was convinced in his own mind that it was merely another hang-out for the Wild Ones, but he wasn't voicing any opinions just then.

That his guess was correct was to be verified much sooner than he expected, and in a way not at all to his liking.

Al Biggers had prepared the noon meal and they were about to eat when they heard the clatter of galloping hoofs. Both outlaws leaped to their feet like startled bucks. Jack Fossum had laid aside his gun belt while he ate, and he swept it up with a single motion which threw it around his waist as he lunged toward the door. Biggers hadn't removed his weapon, and his hand had slapped the handle of the gun at the first alarm.

Right then and there Chet got a glimpse at the hair-trigger existence which these young badmen were compelled to lead. They could on occasion be apparently carefree and happy, but even in their own favorite territory they lived with the knowledge that the heavy hand of the law hung over them like Damocles' sword.

Chet had got to his feet in a more leisurely manner. Like Fossum he had removed his gun for comfort, but not knowing what impended he buckled it on again. As he reached the door Jack Fossum stepped back around the corner of the cabin.

"Keep back," Fossum hissed. "An keep yore head. If they ask you: 'Where's George?' you say: 'In the Bosom of Abraham.'"

Wonderingly, Chet stepped back inside the cabin. He could hear his two companions conferring in low voices, but couldn't hear what they were saying.

By now the approaching horsemen had reached the corral. Peeping out through the single window in the cabin Chet made out four men in the party. They wore typical range garb, and their horses showed that they had been ridden long and hard. As a matter of fact the animals were dead on their feet. A cold, clammy feeling rooted along the cattle buyer's spine. No need to be told what these men were, nor the danger they meant to him.

"Hello, amigos—what's the big rush?" Chet heard Jack Fossum greet the newcomers.

"We're in a tight jam," one of the men replied. "A damned posse is after us for that train robbery at Soldier Summit last fall. Somebody has peached on us. When we rode through Marble canyon this mornin' they were layin' for us. They knew we were comin', an' they knew who it was that pulled the job."

"How'd yuh git away?" Biggers asked.

36

"Bobo rolled his gun on the ox-headed deputy sheriff an' got the drop. They hadda let us go tuh keep him from gittin' killed. But we never got more than a two-mile start," said another man.

"They changed horses at Saddler's ranch, but we didn't have a chance," the first speaker said. "They divided, too, an' one party is headin' through Digger pass. They'll git more fresh horses an' cut us off from reachin' Cattle valley."

"What yuh gonna do, Bobo?" Biggers queried.

"Do?" The other man laughed harshly. "If you fellers ain't got fresh horses for us we'll stick right here an' fight it out. With yore help we kin whip this damned posse behind us, an' one man can hold the trail you come in on if the other bunch gits here. We'll make our gitaway in the night an' hole up in the Stag-tail hide-out till it dies down. They're not gonna stick me away for twenty or thirty years."

"Twenty or thirty years! You'd be lucky, Bobo," said another man. "Me, I'd git sent back tuh Arizona tuh keep a broken date with the hangman down there."

"If I ever find out who tipped off the sheriff about us I'll rip out somebody's black liver," a third man gritted.

"Well, we got no time for that now," said Bobo. "You got anything cooked? All right. We'll eat, an' one o' you boys go back along our trail an' watch for the posse. Shoot twice when yuh see 'em comin'."

By this time the four hard-pressed outlaws had dismounted and were in front of the cabin. Their tired, thirsty horses were already guzzling water at the creek, the men having merely turned them loose with dragging reins.

Never in his life had Chet Kelvin been in a more ticklish situation. He knew that these men would kill him in a second if they suspected that he could stand between them and their liberty. His only chance, he believed, depended upon his two erstwhile companions, and the only way they could save his bacon was to vouch for his being a new member of the Wild Ones. And that might be worse than if they repudiated him altogether. If he went through with it he would have to fight with them against the posse, and that would make him an outlaw in fact as well as by pretension.

It would be fatal, he knew, to display any sign of nervousness. He flung his hat into one corner and busied himself with the cooking. He was juggling a frying pan full of potatoes when the outlaw known as Bobo loomed in the doorway.

"Who the hell is this?" the fellow hissed.

SEVEN

THE EXPRESSION of the outlaw confronting Chet Kelvin from the doorway of the cabin was surcharged with the kind of suspicion that needed but a breath to kindle into sudden and violent action.

With a hostile posse right at their heels the men might be expected to be spooky. But to find that a stranger had just listened to their acknowledgment of guilt was like exploding a firecracker under a bronco colt. Unless the situation was handled with skill something was due to break.

Chet knew that the slightest tremor of fear or look of guilt would be fatal. He might shoot it out with the big outlaw in the door, but he couldn't hope to whip the rest of the pack. He grinned cheerfully.

"Come on in, brother—chuck's ready," he greeted.

The big outlaw remained in the door, his broad thumb holding back the hammer of his half-drawn Colt.

"Who is this rannigan, Biggers?" he repeated.

"That's Chet Kelvin, from up Idaho way," Biggers replied.

"You go watch the trail, Al—I'll do the interducin'," came Jack Fossum's voice, and Chet heaved a sigh of relief. He had been afraid that Jack had been sent back to scout the posse, and he doubted Biggers' ability to handle the situation; even assuming that his intentions were good.

"Go on in, fellers," Fossum continued lightly. "Chet's all tuh the good. I'll vouch for him."

The first danger was past. The big outlaw allowed his six-gun to seek the bottom of its holster as he entered the room. Behind him came another man, bigger and far younger, a fellow of much the same type as Al Biggers, yet so much more brutal in appearance that Biggers instantly leaped into higher esteem in Chet's mind. Behind them came Jack Fossum.

"Chet, I want yuh tuh meet four more of our boys," Jack said. "This"—indicating the older outlaw who had first entered—"is 'Bobo' Waite—the untamed terror of the railroads. This other han'some hombre is the Peace River Kid."

Chet nodded genially, and the Peace River Kid gave him a nod in return, at the same time sizing him up with the furtive curiosity of a jailbird.

Bobo Waite made no sign of acknowledgment whatever.

Now the other two outlaws crowded into the room.

"This is Tony Mex," said Jack Fossum, indicating a dark, slender chap of marked Indian strain. He had a big nose, wide, flaring nostrils, and stooping shoulders from which his long arms hung as loosely as the limbs of a rag doll. He grinned widely.

"This is a pleasure," he assured Chet. "With that posse so damned close I only wish there was a dozen more good men here."

From his voice Chet knew that this was the man who was wanted by the hangman in Arizona.

The fourth outlaw was a mere boy, a tough frontier town kid whose chief characteristic was crass ignorance and an abundance of gall.

"This here is 'Brandy' Waters," Jack finished the introduction.

"Well, don't stand around makin' bows an' bein' polite," Bobo Waite snapped. "Throw some grub into yer guts—it may be the last some o' yuh'll ever git."

The man seized a tin plate and heaped it high with food. Chet saw that somebody was going to go short if the others followed Waite's example.

Chet himself made no effort to eat, nor did Fossum. They had cooked only food enough for three, and the fugitives appeared half famished.

"Where'd yuh pick up this feller, Fossum?" Waite demanded with his mouth crammed full of bacon and hot potatoes.

"We met him over in Curryville, Bobo," Fossum answered.

"Yeah? Ain't knowed him long, huh?" The man's voice bristled with suspicion.

"No, I ain't," Jack said easily. "But I know fellers that has."

"Yeah? Who, fer instance?"

The tense situation which had been temporarily alleviated by Jack Fossum's interference was again a stark reality. It seemed to Chet that he was moving through some sort of an unreal dream; but it was one over which he had no control, and he knew that he must act as the developments decreed.

Unless Jack Fossum managed in some unexpected way to establish his credentials as an outlaw, Bobo Waite and his fellows would act to remove a possible menace to their freedom. And for the life of him Chet couldn't see what Fossum could possibly do. He knew only that if a single one of the outlaws went for his gun he meant to go for his and leave at least one less outlaw for the posse to contend with.

If Jack Fossum was in any way perturbed he showed no sign of it. His engaging grin didn't flicker. He waited for a full minute before answering as though purposely to increase the tension. He certainly realized how Chet must view his predicament.

"What was it yuh asked, Bobo?" he queried innocently. "Oh,

yes, yuh wanted tuh know how Chet happened tuh be with us. Well, he's here on orders from Kirk Holliday."

"Yeah? How do yuh know that?" demanded the suspicious Mr. Waite.

"Kirk told me so," Fossum answered curtly. His manner had suddenly altered. "You've beefed long enough, Bobo," he shot out. "Chet's all right. When Kirk Holliday tells me a man's all right that's good enough for me. If it ain't good enough for you go tuh Kirk about it."

"O' course," Waite said more moderately. "But we're in a tight place an' we never seen this feller before. I just wanted tuh know. If yo're positive that Kirk knows him, it's all right. When did yuh see Kirk?"

"Coupla days ago. Had a long talk with him an' Blackie Payne. They've got a lot o' cattle down here they gotta git rid of some way. Nobody knows Chet down this way is why Kirk sent him down here. By pertendin' tuh be a legitimate cattle buyer he'll be able tuh work a big herd outa here where Kirk couldn't do it himself. Savvy?"

"Shore, shore," Bobo Waite said. He extended a grimy, greasy hand for Chet to shake.

"Excuse my doubts, compadre, but when yuh got a posse hot on yore tail yuh can't take no chances," he said affably.

"Don't I know it," Chet said earnestly. Before he could say more they heard two quick shots.

Bobo Waite rammed half a hot biscuit into his mouth and leaped to his feet. His companions followed his example.

"Git the horses into the stables an' give 'em some hay, Tony," Waite ordered. "The rest of us'll barge back up here on the ridge an' give that posse a reception."

Plainly Chet and Fossum were expected to help fight off the posse. Chet caught the young outlaw's eye for an instant, and Fossum grinned. There could be no holding back.

"You fellers got rifles?" Waite barked.

Both Chet and Jack assured him that they had—on their saddles.

"Git 'em an' come along," the man said tersely. "There's no room for bystanders today."

They hurried out to the haystack and dragged their rifles out of the scabbards. For a moment they were alone.

"Hell of a thing you dragged me into," Chet said bitterly.

"Didn't I warn yuh tuh go back?" Jack retorted. "Yuh can't git away now, an' if that posse licks us there won't be no alibi for you. A bumblebee has got bigger wings than a fly, but that don't do him no good when he gits his feet caught in stick-um paper."

"I'd like tuh turn the whole gang of yuh over tuh that posse," Chet gritted.

"But you won't," Jack murmured. "We're all good fellers. Look at Tony there: you wouldn't like tuh see him hang, I betcha."

"Come on," Chet ground out. "Yore friend Bobo is waitin' for us."

Rifles in hand they joined the outlaw leader. "You two come with me," he said. "I've sent the Kid an' Brandy over tuh side Biggers."

When they reached the top of the ridge back of the cabin Chet could see why the outlaws had located their cabin just where they had. On the other side of the ridge the country sloped away gradually to a bare and treeless flat. The ridge itself formed a triangle, with two prongs running down to meet on the flat. By posting themselves at the top of these prong ridges, back to back, though separated by some three or four hundred yards, the outlaws were able to command a full view of everything on the flat. The same escarpments which walled in the narrow trail over which Chet and his companions had entered kept the posse from executing a flank movement.

Chet saw the posse the moment he reached the top of the hill. The sheriff and his men were congregated at the mouth of a cove on the other side of the flat, half a mile distant. Biggers' shots had apparently caused them to halt and take counsel. Had they known there was only one man on the ridge they could have charged the hill and captured it before the others got there from the cabin. Their golden opportunity had been lost. Now, to gain the ridgetop, they would have to face a devastating fire as they swept across that flat.

The posse was larger than Chet expected. They were in full view and he counted seventeen men.

"Sheriff Jay Wendall is leadin' 'em," Bobo Waite informed Jack Fossum. "That old devil ain't scared o' hell or rattlesnakes. We're gonna have tuh fight."

Even as the outlaw leader was speaking the posse went into action. It divided into two parties. To Chet's surprise one party numbered eleven and the other one six. Instead of charging straight across they circled around the base of the hills; each party going in a different direction. The larger party was the one bent upon the capture of Bobo Waite's ridge.

The eleven men were riding at a fast trot, tandem fashion, with about two rods between the men. At that distance and at that gait they were difficult targets indeed.

Chet was quick to grasp their strategy. The main ridge was higher at the point where the posse would strike it than it was where the outlaws lay. They would be in little danger until they actually reached the foot of the ridge. They couldn't cross it until they got close to where the outlaws hovered, but they would have a downhill sweep, and if it got too hot for them there were numerous boulders and projecting ledges they could use for shelter. While this larger party was attacking here the other men would deploy on the other side and offer a constant threat of attack if that side was left unguarded.

"How yuh fixed fer ca'tridges?" Waite demanded.

"Purty plenty," Fossum answered. "How're you?"

"Plenty forty-fives, but we wasted a lot o' rifle ammunition holdin' that damned posse back," Waite replied. "That's Jay Wendall on lead. If we kin stop him we kin stop 'em all. I don't wanta use my shells till I have to. Try yore marksmanship on him, Kelvin."

Chet sensed that it was a test of him rather than a hope that the sheriff would be killed. If he refused to fire he knew that he could expect to get a bullet in the back the first time it was turned. To comply was definitely to throw in his lot with the outlaws.

All sorts of wild ideas were chasing themselves pell-mell through Chet's brain, and the burden of them all was to seize some favorable opportunity to get the drop on the outlaws and compel the whole kit and kaboodle of them to surrender to the posse. But Bobo Waite's attitude was a portent that no such opportunity was likely to come.

There was still another confusing point in the situation. Fossum and Biggers, particularly the former, had undoubtedly saved his life. Had they not lied for him, Bobo Waite and his allies would have shot him down like a dog. It went against the grain to think of betraying them to the posse. Now that they were actively resisting the law they would be held just as guilty as the others, and no doubt they had plenty of crimes to answer for if they were once caught. But to Chet ingratitude was a major crime.

"Are yuh shootin' or not?" Waite rasped angrily.

Hastily Chet thrust his rifle over a rock and took aim at a spot just back of the sheriff and pulled the trigger. He missed the sheriff, of course. The answer to his bullet was a yell of defiance from the posse.

"Rotten!" Waite breathed in disgust. "I'll see what I can do."

Again Chet's conscience engaged in battle with his judgment. It was his duty as a law-abiding citizen to save the life of the officer if he could. To do so would undoubtedly cost his own.

The range was long, and the odds were ten to one that Waite would miss; but there was that chance that he wouldn't. It was a fact that the sheriff would have been in exactly the same danger if Chet had been a thousand miles from there, but he told himself that that was specious reasoning.

Before he could make up his mind what to do Waite's eye was slanting along his rifle barrel. He was within six feet of the man. Involuntarily he poised himself to leap. Then a sudden gust of wind whipped up a cloud of dust which momentarily obscured the posse. Waite held his fire.

EIGHT

DESPITE a carefully cultivated iron resolution Leda Harrison was at heart a shy girl who loved books and the gentler arts of home-making more than she did rougher and perhaps more exhilarating pleasures. She had undertaken her present adventure with inward trepidation. But for the sake of Bud, as well as for the successful culmination of their undertaking, she had rigidly refused to display any misgivings.

Secretly, however, those misgivings were increasing with every mile and, now that the outcome of the journey was in sight, they had assumed colossal proportions by the time she had finished her interview with Chet Kelvin in Boxtown.

Only her pride and the inherited stoicism of her Yankee forbears prevented her from at least confessing a doubt.

She had changed. Her peach-blossom complexion had darkened to a nut-brown, and her smooth, white fingers were already becoming rough and hard from the unusual tasks of camping out. She refused to sit idly by and allow Nevada to do all the camp chores, for all that he was paid for it. And she kept her rounded little chin up, and insisted that they would either find Charley or learn what had become of him.

In her own mind, however, she recognized dangers which she refused to admit to Bud. The Mormon bishop, Carey, had made her understand that she would find other claimants for the I X L ranch, and she realized that she and Bud hadn't the scratch of a pen that would stand in law, to prove that Charley had ever owned the ranch. All they had was an old letter from Charley in which he had mentioned the big ranch he owned and given a description of some of its features. Her hope was that the burden of proof would somehow fall upon the trespasser in possession, and that he couldn't produce it.

Her brief talk with Chet Kelvin hadn't tended to encourage her. All it proved to her was that Charley Harrison had been in the country. But the intimation that he might be using an assumed name had brought to the foreground of her mind a fear she had with steady persistence refused to admit.

Even yet she dared not let her mind dwell upon that possibility lest circumstances might compel her to accept its truth. That Charley, the gay, handsome, swash-buckling brother she had been so proud of, could be an outlaw—perhaps even one of the notorious Wild Ones about whom he had talked so much—was simply unthinkable. Yet always there was that hazy feeling that Charley had originally left home under a cloud. Why else had his parents so suddenly and unexpectedly retired from all social activities?

"Miss Leda," Nevada said to her, "I ain't runnin' this here outfit, but I shore don't like the way them fellers are hangin' along with us. Don't yuh think it'd be a good idee if we was tuh lay over a day?"

"But why?"

"Wal, they stuck us up once. How do we know they won't do it again?"

"I think we're safe on that score," she smiled. "If two of them were the ones who robbed us, the third one is the man who gave our money back, and they're traveling together."

"Seems almighty quare tuh me," Nevada grumbled. "They must know it was him made 'em give it back. That feller's either an awful fool or dangnation shore of himself. What's tuh hinder them from overpowerin' him, an' then robbin' us again when we come along?"

"We'll have to take that chance, and we must get on," Leda declared.

"You don't need tuh worry about Chet Kelvin," Bud asserted. "He'll take care of himself, and those fellows won't try any more tricks on us while he's with 'em. I hope we meet him again when we get to Highriver."

"We don't know anything about him," Leda warned, but she was conscious of hoping the same thing Bud did. Already she was feeling the need of some dependable friend. Nevada was all right within his limits, but his boundaries were narrow. She really wished she had found some way to be a bit more cordial to Kelvin, but she had been imbued with the idea that he was some sort of an outlaw himself because of his associations with the other two. Bud's contention that he was a cattle buyer was no assurance of honesty, even if true.

It took them nearly three days to drive from Boxtown to the place known as Highriver. They passed a few isolated ranches on the way, but no other towns. The last day they drove for some time beside a turgid, yellowish stream in the bottom of a rock-walled gorge.

"Whoever named this river the High made a mistake," Bud

44

opined. "They should have called it the Low river. It's certainly at the bottom."

"They called it High river 'count o' the way she booms when the floods come, an' believe me they come offen an' they're plenty bad. These mountain cloudbursts kin spill themselves over the flats so fast yuh can't see where they struck till they seem tuh pick up the earth an' bring it right along with 'em. I've seen 'em thunderin' along pushin' a ten-foot wall o' yaller mud in front of 'em. An' when they hit this narrer river gorge she's not only high, she's wide an' han'some," Nevada informed.

"I sure hope one don't strike till we're out of here," Bud said.

"No danger today, an' there's only a few places where a man wouldn't have a chance tuh git out," the guide stated.

It was a little past mid-afternoon when the gorge suddenly widened into a tiny valley. The walls leaned back from the river, and were broken by numerous entering side-canyons. On a low bench between two of these latter, just high enough to be out of danger of the flood zone, stood the little town of Highriver. Its conglomeration of hopeless-looking buildings was built of adobe and unpainted lumber.

As the buckboard jolted along a road that could never be dignified by the title of street, Leda felt a leaden weight inside her breast which threatened to choke her. This drab, desolate, depressing place was then the Mecca of her hopes. She had never felt so pitifully alone and helpless in her life. Only one hope remained; that the I X L ranch would be a brighter oasis.

Nevada stopped the buckboard in front of a long, two-storied building which proved to be a hotel and saloon. A smaller building stood close beside it. This was a store. There were yet other low, squatty buildings in the rear; and still farther behind was a set of corrals and stables.

Leda looked in vain for sight of a church, or even a school-house. Just a little way down the road, however, was a rather neat frame house, well surrounded with trees and vines. At the back was an orchard and garden. On a weather-beaten signboard were the words: POST OFFICE, STORE, MEALS AND LODGING.

Half a dozen rough, lazy-looking characters were loafing in the shade in front of the saloon as the buckboard stopped. They looked up with the naïve curiosity of the rustic, and at sight of a pretty girl one or two of them nudged their fellows.

"This here is Bill Codd's place, Miss Leda, an' I reckon he's the bull-o'-the-woods down this way. It's too late tuh git tuh the I X L tonight, so I reckon we'd better stay here till mornin'.

We kin get grub an' camp like we been doin', or we kin git rooms an' meals," Nevada informed.

Leda was utterly weary of camping out. She longed for a room and a place where she could clean up and wash out some clothing. But Bill Codd's place was repellent to her.

"Drive on to that other place," she ordered quickly.

"Well, all right, but I dunno's it'd be wisdom," Nevada said doubtfully.

"Drive on," Leda commanded curtly.

Nevada picked up his lines and was starting on when an incredibly fat, waddling man with a face as dead looking as that of a freshly killed pig, came out of the saloon.

"Hey, you lookin' for a place tuh stop?" he called.

Nevada halted his team. "Why, yes—" he began.

"Thank you, no," Leda interrupted. "Drive on, Nevada."

The fat man raised a threatening hand, but thought better of it and returned to the saloon. He waddled over to the bar where stood his very antithesis—a lean, angular man whose narrow head was too small to sustain the immense ragged hat he wore; which in consequence came far down over his ears. When he wanted to see anything at a distance it was necessary for him to lift his hat with his hand.

"Well, Adam, I reckon that's the gal that's comin' tuh take yore ranch away from ye," Codd said. "I told ye I'd got word that sech a critter was on the way here a-askin' fer the I X L."

The lean man folded himself over the bar like a jackknife, and the lower half of a leering grin was visible beneath the umbrella-like hat. "I been livin' alone now fer fifty-seven years. I won't mind it a mite havin' a good-lookin' woman about the place," he cackled.

"We gotta find out what she wants an' what she knows," the fat man said. "I wish tuh hell we coulda stopped her from fallin' in with the ole lady Gemmell."

"Bill, thar's only one way yuh'll ever have any peace with Nance Gemmell." Adam Broome laughed. "That's tuh marry her."

"You make my sternum ache," Codd snorted. "I know that old coot drivin' the rig—calls hisself Nevada. Talks all over the place, but never tells nothin'. But I'll find out what's back of it."

As this conversation was going on the buckboard stopped in front of the vine-clad domicile down the road. Leda got out and entered. On her left was a short counter with a few board shelves behind it somewhat denuded of merchandise. She imagined that fifty dollars would be a high price to pay for everything in the place.

On her right was a tiny, boarded-up alcove with a pigeon-

46

hole for the delivery of mail. This was the Highriver post office, which served a back country over two hundred miles deep. The mail came in every ten days.

As Leda was looking around a back door opened and a tall, freckled old woman dressed in the stiffest and starchiest of gingham came in. At sight of the girl the woman scowled. Then she took a longer look and smiled. Her hard, freckled face that had at first seemed forbidding expressed kindness and good cheer.

"How-de-do," the woman greeted. "Anything I kin do for you?"

"I—I'm looking for lodgings for myself and brother," Leda said. "We saw your sign. But if you haven't the rooms we have our own camping outfit."

"Step right this way, miss," the woman invited, and led the way back to a small but scrupulously clean room.

Leda looked at the soft bed with its clean, white linen, at the chintz window curtains, the rocking chair, and old-fashioned lowboy, and it seemed to her that she couldn't stand the discomforts of camping out another night.

"Oh, this will do nicely," she cried.

"There's another room just back of this that'll do for your brother," Mrs. Gemmell said. "How old is he?"

"Sixteen. There is a guide with us, but he'll sleep in his own bed. What we'd like mostly is a bath."

"You'll have to use a tin tub, but I've bathed in one for fifty years, an' I've managed tuh keep the dirt off so far," Mrs. Gemmell grinned. "I'll put the water on right now, an' start somethin' a little extra fer supper. You just make yourself right at home."

"Thank you; but don't go to any trouble," Leda said.

"Don't bother about that. 'Tain't often I have comp'ny an' I appreciate it. Ain't many folks come tuh Highriver that I'd have in my house—an' most o' them stop in Bill Codd's den of iniquity across the street."

"I'm glad I came here," Leda offered.

"So'm I. Pleasure trip?"

"Not hardly," Leda said a little grimly. "We're out here looking for our brother. His name is Charley Harrison. Did you ever hear of him?"

"Harrison? Harrison? No, miss, I can't say I ever did. An' I've lived in this country fer thirty years."

"But he owned the I X L ranch out here," Leda protested. "You must have heard of him."

The woman's expression of kindly interest altered instantly. For a moment it grew tense and hard, and she gazed at the girl searchingly. Then it softened again abruptly.

47

"Well, well, I'd better be gittin' that hot water on," she said cheerfully.

"Just a moment," Leda pleaded. "What about this I X L ranch? Isn't it near here?"

"Yes, it's just fourteen miles northwest o' here."

"We've been told that it is claimed by a man by the name of Adam Broome, but I have a letter from my brother saying it belonged to him. Charley—my brother—seems to have disappeared. That is why we're out here. We fear he has met with foul play."

"Don't you worry, honey," Mrs. Gemmell said kindly. "There's been some sort of a mix-up, but we'll straighten it out all right."

Nancy Gemmell went back into her kitchen, and awakened an old fellow with a sparse white beard who was snoozing in a corner.

"Listen, Leppy," she said. "I see that sorrel horse o' Adam Broome's over in front o' Codd's. I want you tuh go over there an' tell old Adam I wanta see him—now. Come on, stir them creakin' joints o' yours."

NINE

THE WHIRLWIND which had twisted across the flat like a dancing dervish between the sheriff's posse and the outlaws had been a decided advantage to the posse, as well as a god-send to Chet Kelvin. By the time the dust cloud passed, and the twigs and tiny bits of gravel it had picked up had fallen back in its wake, the posse had gained enough ground to enable them to wheel and make an oblique charge toward the ridge at full gallop.

"Give 'em hell!" Bobo Waite ordered excitedly. "We gotta stop 'em before they reach the rocks."

He had no time now to see how Chet behaved, but to avoid arousing his suspicion again, and to make the others think that he was whole-heartedly with them, Chet blazed away right merrily—his bullets going a good ten feet above the heads of the posse.

Out of the corner of his eye Chet saw Jack Fossum firing more deliberately, but nobody fell when he did fire.

But one horse reared, pawed the air frantically, and came down with its forelegs spread wide apart like a drunken man's. It took two or three staggering steps, and then slowly settled to the earth in the same awkward position. Its rider had leaped to the ground before it fell. His companions had already passed him, and he legged it lustily toward the nearest rocks.

Chet watched the man with a somewhat morbid interest, the while he continued to waste good ammunition upon the desert atmosphere. He heaved a sigh of relief when he saw the fellow reach a nest of boulders without attracting another bullet.

But other members of the posse had not fared so well. One man had suddenly slackened his reins and grabbed the saddle horn with both hands. In spite of that he bounced in the saddle like a little boy learning to ride until he collected himself enough to pick up the reins again. He turned his mount off to the left, away from the ridge, and drew it down to a walk. Apparently he had had enough and didn't care who knew it; though he was probably hurt too badly to care about anything else. It took him fifteen minutes to get back to where the posse had started from. All that time he was an easy mark for anybody who might care to shoot at him. But nobody did.

Another man had undoubtedly been wounded by a bullet from Bobo Waite's rifle, but he stayed with his companions until they reached the ridge. Then, evidently at a word of command from the sheriff, the whole party hurled themselves from their horses and took shelter in a sort of swale which transversed the ridge. The edge of the swale was marked by a reef of shale rock which served admirably as a barricade for the posse.

The swale wasn't deep enough for the horses, so the sheriff's men had left the bridle reins hanging over the saddle horns and given the animals a start back across the flat. It seemed an omen of their determination to fight the matter out to a definite conclusion with the outlaws. The released horses, seeing the wounded man riding back the way they had come, naturally followed, with their tails held high, while they swung their heads in the air and snorted loudly. Some of them quickly broke into a gallop.

One of the men in the smaller posse suddenly turned back and galloped fast to head the loose horses in the cove, and perhaps to give aid to the wounded man.

Chet and his two associates were separated from the sheriff's posse by less than three hundred yards.

"Hellish shootin' yuh punks done," Bobo Waite rasped bitterly. "I hit two men an' got a horse, an' none o' the rest of 'em got a scratch."

"Jest wait till we git 'em in six-shooter range," Jack Fossum predicted.

Bobo Waite snorted disdainfully, but his situation was too precarious to allow any time for quarreling. There was no denying that the sheriff had been unexpectedly successful. Chet knew that had two of the others been with Waite in-

49

stead of himself and Fossum, the casualties among the posse would have been far greater. In all likelihood none of them would have reached the ridge.

Now the posse had got down to business. They were firing steadily at the ridgetop, and any man who moved from behind his shelter risked a bullet. One bullet struck the boulder behind which Chet crouched and zoomed away with a disappointed whine. Others were kicking up the gravel on both sides of him. As the possemen moved higher up their swale they were also in a position to make it troublesome for the fellows on the other side of the draw, who were therefore menaced both from in front and from behind. The five men of the other posse were riding back and forth out on the flat, Indian fashion, and keeping up an annoying if not damaging fire.

Bobo Waite was a harried and harassed field marshal. His enemies threatened him, and he felt that his friends had failed him.

"Watch the top o' the ridge," he snarled. "If they git across there they'll cut us off from the cabin, an' be behind us."

And now Chet was compelled to realize the imminent danger of a victory for the sheriff. He had no liking whatever for the prospect of being killed while resisting an officer; and little more for the prospect of being captured as a bandit. His previous clean record and his connections with a big cow outfit wouldn't overcome the damning fact that he had been taken red-handed in the act of assisting a bunch of train robbers to escape.

Now Bobo Waite was shouting for two of the others to come over and join them, and Al Biggers and the Peace River Kid started across the draw, leaving Brandy Waters to deal with the smaller posse alone. Bobo Waite himself withdrew toward the bottom of the draw to meet them.

"Well, how d'ye like it?" Jack Fossum grinned. The next instant he was spitting out dirt which a posseman's bullet had thrown into his mouth as he turned his head.

"Fine," Chet retorted. "Would yuh rather have roses or hollyhocks?"

"A sprig o' sagebrush'll do me," Jack said. "Look out! There's a son-of-a-Ute tryin' tuh sneak over the ridge."

Some fellow obviously was sneaking up the swale on all fours, and naturally that part of his anatomy just below the waist-band of his overalls was the most exposed portion of his body. It was all Chet and Jack could see. The outlaw thrust the barrel of his rifle cautiously forward and pulled the trigger.

Instantly there came an anguished squall, and the posseman leaped suddenly erect. One hand was behind him; the other raised aloft.

Chet heaved a sigh of relief when the fellow presently remembered his circumstances and ducked down out of sight. Chet had learned that Jack Fossum was a mighty fine rifle shot when he wanted to be.

Despite the bullets streaking overhead or kicking up miniature dust spouts about him, Chet was more interested in the doings of the men below him in the draw. They were having an animated discussion, and upon their decision might rest his own fate.

Presently the men separated, and Al Biggers came on toward Chet and Jack. Bobo Waite and the Peace River Kid hurried up the draw toward the top of the ridge.

Jack Fossum emitted an oath under his breath. "I wonder," he said aloud.

"Wonder what?" Chet asked curiously.

"Oh, nothin'," the outlaw said curtly.

They waited impatiently for Biggers to join them. The last few rods he had to crawl to keep under the bullets.

"Where the hell them birds goin'?" Jack shot out.

"To the other side o' the ridge," Biggers stated. "We gotta stop 'em from crossin' the ridge an' gittin' behind us, now that you chumps let 'em git in that close. What the heck was you two shootin' at—the birdies?"

"Never mind that," Fossum grunted. "What's Bobo's plan?"

"It's fer us tuh hold 'em off this way, while him an' Peace River gits over there an' gits above that swale they're in. If they git tuh the top before the sheriff does they kin chase 'em out o' their holes like mice out of a grain box."

"Uh-huh," Jack Fossum grunted.

"Looka here, fellows: I'm willin' tuh be part o' the tail o' those bank robbers' kite along with yuh so long as it's just tuh help 'em fly. But when it comes tuh killin' men I'm out. After all I don't belong tuh the Wild Ones, y' know," Chet said.

"Why didn't yuh say that back in the cabin?" Biggers demanded angrily.

"I'm just tellin' yuh that I'll string along with you boys as long as I can, but I'm not killin' any sheriffs today," Chet retorted sharply.

"I don't think it'd be worth while, either," Jack Fossum said laconically. "They'd only raise a new crop."

Al Biggers snorted with indignation, but before he could think of suitable repartee a bullet slashed through the crown of his hat. He dropped as though he had been really hit. For a moment the others thought he had. He cursed bitterly.

"Now yuh've let one of 'em git above us," he said.

It was indeed a fact. A rifle cracked, and Chet jerked his

leg hastily into a new position. That shot had missed his knee by an inch. It had come from behind a high, protuberant boulder about a hundred and fifty yards distant. One man had got out of the swale; he would keep the besieged hopping while others of the posse advanced.

A rifle barrel suddenly protruded from the side of the boulder, and the desire for self-preservation caused Chet to fire hastily at the rock. Jack Fossum fired at the same instant. The man with the rifle pulled the trigger, but those shots caused him to jerk his gun, and the bullet went high.

By this time Al Biggers had established himself in a relatively safe place, but the man behind the boulder was undoubtedly in a position to make it most bothersome for all three.

Suddenly the firing by the posse ceased. A white handkerchief fluttered over the top of the boulder. Al Biggers would have taken a shot at it had not Fossum restrained him.

"I want tuh talk to you hombres," called the man behind the rock.

"Come out in sight if yuh wanta palaver," Fossum replied.

"Hold yore fire an' I will," the man said. A moment later an erect, brown-faced man with a shaggy, iron-gray mustache stepped from behind the rock.

"Jay Wendall himself," Jack Fossum breathed. "He's that hard a bullet wouldn't hurt him no more than that rock."

"You fellers just as well give in," the veteran sheriff called in bull-bellowing tones. "Yuh'll be cut off the other way, an' we're in position tuh walk all over yuh. No use tuh kill any more men, because yuh can't git away."

"Who's killed any men?" Jack Fossum retorted.

"I don't know, but some o' my men have been shot. But if you don't give up we're comin' in after you."

From where he lay Chet saw a man creeping toward the top of the ridge above where the man had previously got shot in the haunches, but he said nothing. To have done so would have been to endanger the life of the sheriff. A minute more, while the sheriff was still orating, the man crossed the ridgetop, and a moment later a second man followed him. Fossum and Biggers had both been watching the sheriff and had failed to see the men.

"What the hell are you talkin' about?" Jack Fossum called back to the sheriff. "We ain't robbed no bank."

"Then what are you shootin' about?" the sheriff came back.

"Hell, ain't it open season on sheriffs?" Jack demanded. "Don't tell me the season's closed."

"Funny, ain't yuh?" the sheriff said angrily. "Well, I want

52

the whole bunch o' yuh. Better give up now or take the consequences."

To Chet it seemed that a surrender was necessary. Bobo Waite and his partner had failed to stop the possemen from crossing the ridge, and now the tables might be turned at any minute. He knew, however, that it would be unwise for him to make the suggestion. Jack Fossum was thoroughly angry.

"Git back behind that rock, sheriff, we're not bein' took," he called.

"Yo're makin' a mistake," the sheriff warned. "You can't git away. Why compel us tuh kill yuh?"

His answer was a bullet which stirred up the gravel at his feet. The graying officer hopped nimbly back behind his breastworks.

"Let 'em have it, boys," he called to his posse.

A veritable gale of lead whistled over the heads of the three defenders.

"Come on, fellers, we gotta git outa here," Jack Fossum urged. "In five minutes more they'll have us surrounded."

Chet Kelvin was nothing loath to leave his uncomfortable quarters. He followed Fossum, while Al Biggers brought up the rear.

They could see young Brandy Waters busily pumping lead at his section of the posse. Jack waved his hat frantically toward the youth, but couldn't get his eye. Then he raised his rifle and placed a bullet neatly in the top of an ant hill two feet from the young outlaw's face. That got his instant and profane attention. As he looked around Jack waved his hat for him to come on.

They could walk until they were almost to the top of the draw, and by stooping low they could avoid being seen by the sheriff and his men, but the other party, though much farther away, could see them plainly. As they crossed over the ridge Chet glanced back and saw the five men who were still mounted suddenly come charging in at full speed.

"Where the hell is Bobo an' the Kid?" Biggers demanded querulously.

The question went unanswered, but the two possemen who had crossed the ridge were promptly heard from. One of them sighted the fugitives, and with a whoop opened fire.

By this time Chet and his comrades were so used to being fired at that they didn't trouble to see where the bullets went. But at this sign of discovery they bounded for the nearest shelter.

This side of the ridge, fortunately, was covered with brush and small trees right down close to the cabin.

"Where the hell is Bobo an' the others?" Biggers complained again.

They waited for a minute or so for Brandy Waters to join them. He was panting from a hard run, and shaking blood from a bullet-scratch across the back of his hand.

"Where we goin' now? Where's the others?" he demanded.

"Take a look," Jack Fossum said bitterly, pointing a finger toward the lower end of the hay meadow, beyond the cabin.

There, just disappearing behind a hill, and riding at a fast lope, were Bobo Waite and the Peace River Kid. They were mounted upon the horses of Biggers and Fossum.

Chet didn't need to be told that the other outlaw, Tony Mex, was already far ahead of those two on his Mike horse.

"That's the way they was gonna drive the sheriff outa that swale," Jack told Biggers cynically. "Beat it as fast as their legs would carry 'em tuh git our horses."

"Why, the dirty—" A stream of blasphemy issued from Al Biggers' mouth.

"An they lef' me behind! Why, damn their souls if I ever git a chance at them I'll cut their rotten hearts out an' split 'em before their faces," Brandy Waters raved in helpless anger.

There were four completely given out horses down at the corral, which it would be a waste of time to mount. And behind them was a sheriff's posse, eager for action, which now had all the advantage of position.

"Well," Chet queried with grim humor, "where do we go from here?"

TEN

ANY EFFORT to escape upon the exhausted horses of the four outlaws would certainly have been wasted effort. They would be overhauled or shot down before they could go a mile.

Jack Fossum, now that he knew he was cornered, was grimly philosophical. Al Biggers was defiant, and obviously scared. Young Brandy Waters relieved his feeling by an incessant stream of profanity directed at his former associates.

"If I ever git one o' them stinkin' polecats lined over the sights o' my gun I'll sink 'em like a ship," was the burden of his song.

"We ain't got time tuh be tellin' what we'll do tuh them when we ketch 'em," Jack Fossum snapped. "We got plenty on our hands right now without tryin' tuh read the stars."

54

"It looks like there was nothing to do but surrender." Chet shrugged.

They were hustling through the brush toward the cabin, and were temporarily screened from the posse. The latter knew that they had only to move warily through the timber in order to drive the bandits into the cabin or out into the open.

"I'm sorry we dragged you into this, Chet," Jack Fossum said.

"Aw, tuh hell with him," Al Biggers growled.

"Shut your trap," Fossum snapped. "It won't help us a damned bit tuh git Chet in bad. We're gonna give him a chance tuh git away."

"How d'ye mean?" Biggers demanded.

"They ain't got a good look at him yet, an' if we can git into the cabin without him bein' seen we kin fix it." Fossum hurriedly outlined his plan. Biggers listened dubiously, while Brandy Waters stared in bewilderment.

"We kin try it," Biggers conceded reluctantly, "but I'm damned if I know why we should."

"Yuh mean tuh say that this hombre don't run with the Wild Ones?" Waters blurted.

"Of course he does," Fossum said impatiently. "It just happens they don't know him down here. Maybe he'll git a chance tuh let us loose."

Chet said nothing. He doubted if the sheriff could be fooled, but Fossum's scheme seemed worth trying—and he had no wish to be branded as an outlaw.

While the three outlaws retreated slowly through the small patch of timber, keeping up a steady but impotent fire all the while, Chet hurried on ahead and got into the cabin as inconspicuously as possible.

Ten minutes later he was joined by the other three.

"Hold that damn' posse back a few minutes longer," Fossum requested the other two. He at once went to work and tied Chet hand and foot with a rope, anchored him to a bunk at one end of the cabin and inserted a gag in his mouth.

Before he had finished the mounted possemen had swooped down around the lower side of the cabin and cut off their retreat. The others were firing steadily at the cabin from the fringe of timber.

"Better stick up a white rag before somebody gits killed," Jack Fossum suggested. A minute later he stuck a more or less white dishrag out of the window on the end of his rifle barrel and waggled it frantically. A few minutes later Sheriff Wendall walked toward the cabin. He halted fifty yards away.

"I ain't standin' fer no more trickery," he yelled. "You fel-

55

lers come outa there with yore hands up. If one o' yuh makes a false move my men'll mow yuh down like grass."

"Comin', sheriff," Jack Fossum replied, and walked out with his hands in the air. The other two followed.

"Where's the others?" the sheriff demanded.

"Sorry, sheriff, but there ain't no more," Fossum grinned.

"Keep these men covered, boys," the sheriff said to his possemen. "I'm goin' into that cabin. If anything happens let these fellers have it like they was mad dogs—which they are."

A moment later Chet saw the sheriff standing in the door of the cabin. He did his best to get out a groan, but the effort resulted only in a choked gurgle. Jack Fossum had done a good job with his gag.

"What the hell?" Sheriff Wendall blurted. He strode over and removed the gag from Chet's mouth. "Who're you?" he demanded.

It was a minute before Chet could answer.

"I'm a cattle buyer for the Idaho Land and Livestock Company," he explained. "I was on my way tuh look at some cattle with two fellows, and we'd got this far when four men rode in an' said they was bein' chased by a posse. They tied me up this way an' went away. That's all I know."

"Sounds likely," the sheriff scoffed with obvious disbelief. "Got any credentials?"

"In my coat."

The sheriff searched his pockets and found papers and a draft book which corroborated Chet's story.

"This seems dang queer," the officer frowned. "It's plain that these fellows out here tried tuh hold us back so the worst ones o' that train robbin' gang could make a gitaway on fresh horses. But I'm damned sure there was seven men come over that ridge."

"I've told yuh all I know," Chet said.

The sheriff called his men together.

"So you pulled a trick, didn't yuh?" he addressed the three outlaws in general, and Jack Fossum in particular. "Let Bobo Waite, Tony Mex, an' the Peace River Kid git away on yore horses, figgerin' we didn't have so much on the rest of yuh. Well, yuh'll find I've got plenty on yuh before yuh git outa the pen. I'm arrestin' yuh now for interferin' with the officers o' the law an' attempted murder."

"Aw, come off, Wendall," Jack said. "We didn't know they was bank robbers, an' we didn't know who you was. An' we didn't give 'em our horses—they took 'em."

"You can tell that to a jury," the sheriff snapped. "I'm out tuh run you Wild Ones outa my county or put yuh behind bars, an' I figger I've made a dang good start. What about that man in the cabin?"

"Just a pilgrim cattle buyer," Jack answered carelessly. "We didn't want him tuh git hurt, an' we didn't want him hurtin' us, so we tied him up."

The sheriff walked over and unfastened the rope which bound Chet.

"I reckon yo're all right," he said, "but better remember the story of old dog Tray. You been travelin' in darn' bad company."

"What about the ones who got away?" a posseman asked.

"If the other posse don't head 'em off they'll git away—this time," the sheriff said. "But I've got a hunch I know where they're headin'. It ain't in my county so I can't take a posse, but I may take a personal pasear over that way a little later."

"Better be careful sheriff," a man advised. "The Wild Ones are out tuh lift yore scalp."

Chet was beginning to admire this grizzled, courageous officer of the law. He had already learned that few sheriffs were eager to antagonize Kirk Holiday and his gang.

Presently the men who had been wounded were brought in, and one of them, the man who had turned back, was in terrible pain. His condition increased the ire of the possemen. This posse was largely made up of ranchers and cowboys who had suffered from the depredations of the Wild Ones. Certain dark and lowering looks, and muffled murmurings let the prisoners know that a time-honored method of summary dealing with outlaws was receiving a measure of consideration. Nothing came of it, however. Sheriff Wendall was a man of force and they knew that no such action would be tolerated by him.

The remainder of the posse came stringing into the hideout before dark, and in consideration of the lateness of the hour and the condition of the horses, the sheriff announced that they would all remain at the cabin until morning.

No two of the prisoners were allowed to sleep together that night, but before supper the handcuffs were removed, and they were not restored. That night as Chet lay awake, thinking of his position, he called himself all sorts of a fool for having yielded to the impulse to become the associate of outlaws; but whenever he thought of the buckboard girl and her brother he couldn't regret that he had come into the country, and his ultimate destination was still the I X L. Moreover, he wanted to help Jack Fossum get out of the scrape if possible. For all the young outlaw's wild ways Chet couldn't believe that he was criminally-minded.

Outlaws and possemen alike were eating breakfast together

shortly after daybreak. The tenseness of the previous day had departed. There was considerable good-natured banter passed back and forth. The wounded men were all better, and able to be moved. To all appearances this might well have been a round-up crew, eating hurriedly to get ready for a big day's gather.

When breakfast was over the prisoners were ordered to mount. Chet sensed that there was imminent danger that either Al Biggers or Brandy Waters would yet give him away. The outlaws were sullen and resentful of the fact that he was at liberty. Moreover, they knew he had had quite a long private talk with the sheriff that morning.

The sheriff had really only wanted to find out how much Chet was willing to swear against the prisoners. Whether wisely or not, Chet had disclaimed knowledge that his companions were outlaws until they tied him up. To have done otherwise would have compelled him to take the stand and swear to things which would surely have destroyed any chance that Fossum and Biggers might have. And Jack Fossum had certainly saved his life and probably kept him out of jail.

His own horse having been stolen, Chet was permitted to take one of the animals which the outlaws had ridden the day before. The animal couldn't possibly recover from that long, grueling ride in a day, and it was doubtful if it ever would. It was better than being afoot, and that was all that could be said for it.

"Well, Kelvin," the sheriff said, "you can ride back tuh Newdale with the posse if yuh want to; but I'd advise yuh not tuh try tuh buy any cattle in this country unless yuh can git together a hard-ridin', hard-fightin' bunch o' men yuh can depend on. Otherwise, yuh'll be out yore time an' money."

"I suppose yo're right, sheriff, but I lost the best horse I ever owned yesterday, an' I'm stickin' in this country until I know I can't git him back."

"Got an idee where yuh might find that said horse?" the sheriff asked shrewdly.

"No; but I've got an idea I may find out."

"Well, suit yoreself," the sheriff said shortly. "I've got no reason tuh make yuh go back."

Chet stood by the outlaw cabin and watched the posse and prisoners ride away. He wanted to say good-bye to his friend Fossum but knew that it would never do. He couldn't tell now just how skeptical Sheriff Wendall was of his status, but he knew that the officer suspected the traditional colored gentleman somewhere in his legal woodpile.

When the others were out of sight he slowly mounted the horse the murderer, Tony Mex, had exchanged for old Mike.

He rode slowly back through the gap by which he had entered the place, for the horse's legs were as stiff as broom handles.

In the course of an hour or so the animal limbered up a bit, but Chet had to ride at a slow gait. It seemed rather pathetic that he should attempt to overhaul the fast-riding bandits on such an animal, but he knew that there was a hide-out of the Wild Ones on Stag-tail butte, and Jack Fossum had told him how to get there. Bobo Waite and his companions were as likely to go there as anywhere else, and if he didn't find them there he still might find out something about Charley Harrison, alias Dude Johnson.

ELEVEN

WHILE Leda Harrison was luxuriating in a hot bath, and it was luxury despite the fact that it was taken in a tin tub on a kitchen floor, her hostess was engaged in earnest conversation out in the front room with Adam Broome.

The man had been little less than dumfounded when Mrs. Gemmell's messenger, the innocuous old fellow known as "Leppy" because of his pathetic resemblance to an orphaned calf, had informed him that she wanted to see him.

"Wal, I'll be eternally rolled up like a hoop!" he ejaculated. "Nance Gemmell wants tuh see me. What yuh make o' that, Bill?"

"Best way tuh find out is go see her," Bill Codd advised. "Ain't skeered o' her, are yuh?"

"I suttinly am," the lengthy one admitted. "Too skeered tuh go, an' afeared tuh stay away. Nance ain't spoke tuh me fer twenty years, but I'm bettin' she'll make up fer all that lost time at one sittin' if she once starts talkin'."

"It's somethin' tuh do with that gal," Codd said. "Better find out what it is."

Thus it was that Adam Broome crossed the street and timidly approached the house of the widow Gemmell. She was waiting for him with a grim expression which did nothing to allay his fears.

"Hoddy, Nancy, hoddy," he said too effusively, and removed his huge and battered hat, thereby exposing a bald dome which ran up to a peak like a mountain above timber line.

"Come in here, Adam Broome," the widow said grimly. "I want tuh talk tuh you."

"Yeah, that's what I understood from Leppy," the man said. Had he been a dog he would certainly have been wagging his tail while he crawled forward on his belly.

59

Mrs. Gemmell stepped behind her counter, and planted her two work-roughened hands firmly upon the boards.

"Adam, I want tuh know who the I X L belongs to," she announced.

"Why, Nancy, I thought yuh knowed that after Martin died I got a-holt of it, an'—"

"Don't lie tuh me, Adam Broome," the woman said. "Think I didn't git acquainted with you in the ten years yuh worked fer my husband on the I X L? If they was sellin' ranches at ten cents an acre you never coulda raised money enough tuh buy a buildin' spot."

"Aw, Nancy, I ain't that profligate," Adam demurred. "I'm savin', I am. I was just sowin' my wild oat crop when I worked fer Martin."

"Yuh sowed wild oats an' yo're still reapin' thistles," Mrs. Gemmell said. "Martin Gemmell was foreman of the I X L for ten years. I knew what it was worth. I know it was worth more money than you could ever raise in spite o' the way them rustlers looted it after they murdered Martin."

The woman's voice had developed a tone that was hard as iron and cold as ice. Adam Broome writhed in spirit, while he nervously twirled his big, ragged hat around and around on one skinny finger.

"I don't say you had anything tuh do with Martin's murder," Mrs. Gemmell went on. "You were too good-natured fer that. In fact, that's just yore trouble—you let yoreself be used for a tool by anybody that'll buy you a few drinks an' pat yuh on the back."

"Aw, Nancy—!" the unhappy culprit pleaded.

"You stayed on the I X L after Martin was killed an' you made no protest against the way things were goin'," the woman went on. "An' when the folks who owned it were persuaded that it could never be made tuh pay an' sold it fer half what it was worth you was the dummy for whoever bought it. An' yuh been a dummy ever since. You claim tuh own the best ranch in the country yet you can't even buy yoreself a new hat. You've worn that fer seven years tuh my certain knowledge."

"Aw, now, I'm jest fond o' this here hat," Adam protested, as he tried vainly to conceal the offending skypiece behind his all too thin body.

"What I want tuh know now is who are you dummy for? Who actually owns the I X L? I wanta know it bad or I'd never have lowered myself tuh speak tuh yuh," Mrs. Gemmell said.

For the first time Adam Broome showed a flash of spirit.

"If I ain't good enough tuh speak to I ain't good enough tuh pass out free information," he declared sulkily.

"Listen, Adam," Mrs. Gemmell said in a quiet voice, "a nice girl has just arrived here. She thinks the I X L belongs to her brother. I don't know who he is, but I suspect he's just some prodigal son who's joined the Wild Ones. Whoever he is he's been makin' tall talk to his folks. This girl is fine. It'd break her heart tuh find out her brother was an outlaw. If I can help it she never will find out. She's goin' out there tomorrow an' you're goin' to make her welcome."

"But I can't tell her her brother ever owned the place."

"You kin do just that," the woman disputed. "You can tell her that you did sell out to her brother, an' that you're just runnin' the ranch in his absence."

"But, hell's-fire, I can't do that," Adam protested.

"Because yo're afraid of the man who actually does own the outfit, eh? That's why I wanta know who that man is."

"It's in my name," Adam asserted.

"I know. But you have tuh do whatever he wants because he has somethin' on you. Well, you'll be worse off than that if you don't do what I say," Mrs. Gemmell said grimly. "You'll tell her that, an' then we'll git busy an' find out which one of the worthless young devils of Kirk Holliday's Wild Ones is her brother, an' we'll make him show up here as owner if he can, or if not a deal can be fixed up so she'll think he couldn't pay you, an' you had tuh take the place back. But you can see that this brother of hers gits enough money to take care of her."

"Nancy, yo're the last woman on earth I ever thought would go crazy," Adam Broome said mournfully.

"Crazy, am I?" The woman bristled. "If I'm crazy it's because I've stayed here all these years firm in the faith that some day I'd find out who it was that murdered my husband. I've always suspected that you knew who it was."

"Honest, Nancy, I was all broke up when Martin got killed," the man said.

"But you went right on associatin' with his murderers. That's why I've had no use for you. But I've got use for you now. I've seen too many young lives busted in this outlaw country. You're gonna help me protect this girl an' her brother."

"I'm afraid I can't obleege ye, Nancy." Broome shrugged.

"But you're goin' to, Adam," the woman said with a grim smile. "I liked you well enough one time, Adam, an' then I come tuh despise yuh. But as the years passed I become more charitable. I saw that you couldn't no more help bein' what you are than a fawn kin help its spots. That's the only reason I didn't git my revenge when I had the chance."

"What yuh mean, Nancy?" the man asked anxiously.

"About two years ago, Adam, Sheriff Jay Wendall had a battle with a bunch of Kirk Holliday's outlaws not far from here. One of 'em was wounded. He was just a kid, an' he'd been workin' out at the I X L for quite a while. You remember him? His name was Walton. For some reason the Wild Ones called him 'Jap.' "

Adam Broome's face had become strained. "He died," he whispered.

"Yes; he died in this house. He escaped the sheriff and he tried to make it to the I X L, but he fainted an' fell off his horse right back of my place. Leppy found him the next mornin' an' we got him in here. I done all I could for him, but he was dyin' an' he knew it. He wanted a priest, but o' course there wasn't any. So he done the next best thing an' confessed his sins tuh me."

The old lady stopped impressively.

"What's the matter, Adam—yuh got the ague?" she queried.

"What did he say?" Adam said huskily.

"He told how he'd met Kirk Holliday an' other outlaws at the I X L, an' how they persuaded him tuh join up with 'em, an' he told of a few petty little jobs they'd let him help with. Oh, his crimes didn't amount tuh much, an' I reckon he didn't write out nothin' about Kirk that everybody don't know. What was really new was what he said about you, Adam. It proved that the I X L has been a headquarters for the Wild Ones for years."

"Yuh say he wrote it out?" Adam whispered.

"Yes. I'll show it to you. Poor kid, he was so weak that he had tuh stop every few lines, but he said it was worth it all when he finally got it down an' off his conscience. He insisted that me an' Leppy sign it as witnesses."

Broome let his fascinated gaze dwell fearfully upon the document which she held out.

"Not knowin' everything I'm afraid he thought you was a bigger villain than you are," Mrs. Gemmell consoled. "But Jay Wendall would give his right eye tuh git his hands on this paper. He's been tryin' for years tuh git something definite on you an' Bill Codd."

"Why ain't yuh done give it to him before this, Nancy?" the man asked.

"If I'd have got this ten years ago I'd have certainly turned it over," the woman said. "But I've come tuh have a measure of charity an' tolerance in my old age. I knew that you was the only one that could be made tuh suffer by it, an' I lost my desire tuh hurt yuh years ago. You are a likable old wretch in spite of yuh bein' so blamed weak an' ornery."

"Then—then you ain't hated me like I thought yuh did," he said eagerly.

The woman had been betrayed into a certain softness. Now her manner altered swiftly.

"Don't think yore danger is past, Adam Broome," she said fiercely. "Either you help me help this girl an' tell me who is really the boss of the I X L or this paper goes into Jay Wendall's hands the first time I see him."

Adam's clawlike fingers clasped and unclasped nervously. "I—I'll do what I kin, Nancy," he promised, "but don't ask me tuh name that man. What this confession o' Jap's kin do tuh me ain't nothin' tuh what he kin do."

"I'll make this agreement with yuh, Adam," Mrs. Gemmell offered. "I'll promise not tuh make no use of the information yuh give me if it can be avoided. But that'll mean you'll have tuh do somethin' besides bein' a doormat. I'd advise yuh tuh swaller a few ramrods tuh reinforce yore backbone."

Adam Broome stepped to the door and cast a frightened glance all around. Then he came back to the counter in front of Nancy.

"Before God, Nancy, I swear that I never had a thing tuh do with Martin Gemmell's death. But I was a dupe like I guess I've always been. I tolled Martin to his death. He believed I'd done it on purpose, an' he lived long enough tuh accuse me. He wrote it on the back of an old envelope. Bill Codd was the first man tuh find the body, an' instead o' turnin' over the envelope he done like you did with this confession o' Japs—he kept it."

The man suddenly broke down and sprawled awkwardly across the counter. His bony frame was racked with sobs.

The widow's eyes filled with pity as she patted him lightly on the shoulder.

"Poor Adam," she murmured. "The trouble with you is you're just like a lubberly Percheron colt tryin' tuh run with a bunch of mustangs. You just ain't fast enough."

"All these years I've been scared tuh death that'd come out." The man wept. "I couldn't bear the idee that you'd think I'd killed Martin, an' the way yuh acted let me know you suspected me anyway. If that letter ever showed up with Martin accusin' me his own self nothin' would ever change yore mind."

"So it *is* Bill Codd who owns the I X L?" the woman mused. "I've suspected that all the time. An' he's hand in glove with the Wild Ones. I've known that, too."

"But nobody kin prove it," Adam said. "He's allus made me be the go-between. You can see yoreself how young Jap

Walton was fooled. An' even the deeds are all in my name. We couldn't prove nothin' on Codd."

"Well, you go back there an' tell that fat gorilla that you've invited this girl an' her brother out tuh the ranch, an' you be darned certain that no harm comes to 'em. If Bill Codd objects to it you let me know." Mrs. Gemmell dismissed him.

By that time Leda was out of her tub. She wore a satin kimono, her hair was brushed back and collected in a great golden coil at the nape of her neck, and there were roses in her cheeks to rival any in Nancy Gemmell's flower garden.

"Well, how d'ye feel now, miss?" Nancy asked.

"I feel great," Leda said. "You're awfully kind to make everything so comfortable for us."

"Oh, that's nothin'," Nancy said lightly. "An' I got some good news for you."

"Good news?"

"Yes. I've just been talkin' with Adam Broome, the man who runs the I X L for your brother."

"Then, then Charley is out here!" Leda exclaimed joyously.

"Now, don't you go gettin' excited," Nancy smiled. "Your brother bought the I X L all right, but that don't mean he's got it paid fer. As a matter o' fact he ain't. An' he's back East somewhere tryin' tuh raise money. In the meantime Adam Broome, the man he bought it from, is runnin' it for him."

"Oh!" Leda could not restrain her keen disappointment. "I wonder why he didn't write. If we'd only known he was in the East—"

"That's easy," Nancy said. "He has prob'ly been too worried about money matters tuh write, an' likely he figgered on surprisin' you with a visit."

"Yes, that's probably true," Leda admitted.

"An' now you've got a chance to surprise him. You just stick right here with me till he shows up."

"That's awfully kind of you, but we'll just go out to the ranch and wait for him," Leda said firmly.

TWELVE

It was almost dark that night when Chet Kelvin came in sight of a small mountain ranch. He had been climbing steadily all day as fast as his stiff-legged mount could navigate, and it was wild, rough country in which he found himself.

A small meadow, or park, watered from the seep of invisible

springs, afforded an excuse for there being a ranch at this particular spot. The house was but a shack, and the outbuildings a mere contraption of poles and old slabs. Chet needed but a single glance to know that prosperity did not abide here.

He strongly suspected that Kirk Holliday himself might have planted some hanger-on of his gang, not able to ride with the Wild Ones, to operate this place as a station for his men in time of need.

At his shout a dejected-looking specimen with a long, drooping mustache and hopeless shoulders came to the door.

"Howdy," Chet greeted. "What's the chance tuh stay all night?"

"Does this look like a hotel?" the man demanded grouchily.

"It looks all right tuh me," Chet said bravely. "All I want is somethin' tuh eat an' a place tuh turn my horse."

The homesteader turned his rheumy eyes upon Chet's horse, and betrayed himself into a show of interest.

"Yuh been ridin' purt' damned hard, looks like," he ventured.

Chet decided to take a chance. "Who wouldn't—with a posse on his tail."

"Posses must be gettin' dangnation thick in these parts," the fellow said. "Had another bunch wanta stop with me last night that was bein' chased by a posse. But they was a sight better mounted than you be."

"It was the same posse," Chet said. "The other boys got some fresh mounts, but I got cut off an' didn't git one."

"That so? Where's George?" the man blurted.

Just in time Chet remembered the words Jack Fossum had told him to use if asked this particular question. "In the Bosom of Abraham." He grinned, and rather hoped that it might be true. "Well, do I git some supper or no?"

"I reckon so," the man said grudgingly. "Only, if any posse shows up don't you bear down none on me."

"No danger of that," Chet assured. "Besides, I throwed that posse off the trail hours ago."

"Well, turn yore horse in the fiel', an' make yoreself at home," the man directed. "Yuh ain't gonna find anything palatial around here. Ever' time I git somethin' ahead you dang outlaws come along an' eat me out of it."

"I'm payin' for anything I git," Chet said. "That's a likely-lookin' little cayuse there in the corral. How much boot would you take?"

"Wouldn't sell that little roan pacer fer love ner money," the man said, but he led the way out to the corral.

The horse which had caught Chet's eye was small, but he was in good condition, and he looked tough and wiry. They haggled until dark, with the result that Chet became the owner of the roan pony for sixty dollars in cash. He agreed to leave the horse he had ridden, but he refused to give a bill of sale.

They were eating supper by the light of a small coal-oil lamp with a smoky chimney when they heard a shout outside. The host sprang up in alarm.

"Wonder who that kin be?" he hissed. "If it's a posse yuh take yore medicine if yuh git ketched. But there's a trap door here that connects here with a 'tater pit which has an openin' at the back if yuh wanta take it."

"Don't worry about me," Chet smiled.

The homesteader went out, and a moment later Chet heard a strangely familiar voice, though he was unable to remember where he had heard it. Stepping to the door he saw three men coming in. He immediately retired to his seat at the table, but he shifted his holster around so that he could get at his gun handily.

"Yuh say yuh've already got a visitor, an' yuh don't know who he is?" the vaguely familiar voice asked.

"That's right, Kirk. But he was ridin' a give-out hawse an' he had the password, so I couldn't turn him off."

The door was flung open, and the next moment Chet saw the blond young giant whom he had encountered at Hopkins' ranch standing in the doorway. He was followed by his dark little lieutenant.

"Well, I'm a cross-eyed Injun if it ain't the cattle buyer," the light-haired outlaw ejaculated. "What the hell are you doin' here?"

Chet had had an instant to prepare himself after he had heard the homesteader call this man Kirk. Enlightenment had flooded his mind. This man, who had called himself Hank Stevens, could be nobody but the famous Kirk Holliday himself. Chet had instantly decided that his best course was to tell the unadulterated truth.

"Howdy, Kirk," he grinned, rising and extending his hand.

Kirk Holliday ignored the outstretched hand. He stepped swiftly to one side, and Chet saw the small, dark man's hand drop to the handle of his gun like a striking rattler. Holliday's baby-blue eyes were hard and cold.

"What's the idea, Kelvin?" he asked.

"The idea? Why, didn't you invite me to Stag-tail butte?"

"I didn't invite no damned detective there," the outlaw chief rasped. "Keep him covered, Blackie. Grant, you git his gun."

For an instant Chet was tempted to make a fast draw and shoot it out with the two outlaws, but he wisely realized that Blackie Payne, whom he now knew the small man to be, would get in the first shot.

The homesteader walked around and got his gun. Chet placed both elbows on the table and rested his chin upon his hands.

"Where do you get that detective stuff, Holliday?" he asked evenly.

The outlaw chief pulled back a chair and seated himself. The others did likewise. "First thing you do is stick up two of my best men an' take their swag away from 'em right on the job. But gettin' them two boys arrested an' almost landin' another bunch right on top of that was what I'd call a master-piece."

"What?" Chet blurted.

"You overlooked the fact that the Wild Ones have a lot of eyes all over this country," Holliday answered. "One of my men was ridin' with the sheriff's posse all the time, an' I got word of what happened at the Shell creek hide-out almost as soon as it happened."

This, certainly, was something Chet hadn't figured on. He knew that Holliday would be suspicious of his motives when he had started for Stag-tail butte, but it had never entered his mind that he would be suspected of being an emissary of the law.

But as he looked at it now he realized that the outlaws blamed somebody for having brought the sheriff onto their trail, and his actions, from their viewpoint, were indeed suspicious. True, Jack Fossum could vouch that he had been led instead of leading into the path of the posse—but Jack himself was in jail.

"I didn't expect the great Kirk Holliday tuh go into hysterics," Chet said calmly. "I really figgered yuh had a head on yore shoulders."

"What d'ye mean?" Holliday asked dangerously.

"You figgered I was sap enough tuh let yuh git yore hands on a big wad of money. Now you find I won't do that you imagine I'm smart enough tuh tell the sheriff just where you an' yore men will be, for all that I've never been in the country before."

"I don't know you've never been here before," Holliday denied. "An' I don't figger yo're alone. You've got one of my men tuh double-cross me. But I'm tellin' yuh now, Kelvin: if I ever find out who that man is he'll never squeal on anybody else."

"Then what do you do tuh men who sneak away when a fight is goin' on, steal their friends' horses, an' leave them tuh fight a posse on foot?"

67

"Who done that?" Holliday demanded.

Chet seized the opportunity to give his version of what had taken place. Blackie Payne was openly incredulous, but Holliday himself was a little less assured.

"An' so you headed for Stag-tail alone, with the idee that you could make Tony Mex give up that glass-eyed horse of yores, huh?" he asked with some amusement.

"That's the general idea," Chet admitted.

"We'll see how it works out," Holliday said. "Fix us some supper, Grant."

Chet had known that he was in some danger when in the company of Al Biggers and Jack Fossum, but that was nothing compared with his present association with Holliday and Payne. He had heard that Holliday wasn't a wanton killer, but the man wouldn't hesitate to take life if he thought his own safety was threatened. In fact his sardonic sense of humor was such that Chet realized that even if he got away with his life he would no doubt suffer some unpleasant irritations.

There was no doubt whatever that Bobo Waite would seize upon the opportunity to denounce him in order to justify his own base desertion of his companions.

For all that Kirk Holliday appeared entirely careless in his movements Chet knew that the outlaw chief was like a purring tiger. One instant he could be apparently playful as a kitten; the next would find his claws unsheathed, and his teeth bared. And the lynx-eyed Blackie Payne didn't relax his watch upon Kelvin for even a moment. It would be impossible to escape from those two for the present.

Chet almost wished he had chosen the potato pit exit which Grant had told him about. Holliday seemed to read his mind, for he ordered Grant to make a bed over the trap door.

There being no chance to escape, Chet resolved to make the best of it and he slept soundly all night. In the morning they had an early breakfast, got in the horses, and no objection was offered when Chet threw his saddle upon the roan pony.

"Make that cayuse keep up if it kills him," Holliday said tersely. That was the only threat or order given.

Chet observed that Blackie Payne had thrust the gun he had taken into his chaps pocket, and Payne always managed to ride behind. For the most part Chet rode abreast of or just behind Holliday. The outlaw chief wasn't bad company. He talked horse mostly, but never a word as to what he intended to do to Chet.

They had no reason to complain of the roan pony. It was tough as whalebone, and there wasn't a lazy bone in its body. Chet continually had to hold it down to stay even with the outlaws. He had a deep-seated idea that Blackie Payne would welcome the opportunity to sink a bullet into him if he even looked as if he might be going to attempt to escape.

It was high noon when they rode into Kirk Holliday's temporary headquarters camp in an aspen-covered draw beside a small, silvery creek. This was a high, mountainous country far from even the nearest isolated Mormon settlement. It was a marvelous range country with grass enough for ten times the number of cattle there seemed to be. Chet wondered if the owners of the cattle he saw had any idea that the Wild Ones were quartered upon their domain. He was soon to find out.

There seemed to be nearly a score of outlaws at this camp. They appeared to be carrying on the usual occupations of an idle cow outfit at the time. A few were playing cards, four were pitching horseshoes, but most of them were engaged in repairing gear. One was even reading a book. But at the approach of their chief they all crowded around. Among them were the three bandits Chet had recently encountered.

For the most part these men were young. Their lean, sun-browned faces were hard, and some of them wore an air of reckless bravado a bit too conspicuously. But few of them looked to be out and out degenerates. In Chet's estimation Bobo Waite was the most evil-looking of them all.

The outlaws themselves, even Kirk Holliday, might have been surprised had they known that Chet Kelvin had spent ten years of his life on the long cattle trails from Texas to the Northwest, and had made his name a synonym for courage along those routes. Only he hadn't been known as Chet Kelvin along those trails. His nickname there had been "Tornado Tex." Chet didn't like it, and he went by his rightful name whenever possible. But had he spoken that name, he knew that most of the outlaws present would have heard of him before.

"Hi, Kirk. Hi, Blackie," a young outlaw greeted. "What yuh got there, a mascot?"

"Mebbe," Holliday grinned.

Chet had noticed Bobo Waite, Tony Mex, and the Peace River Kid go into a huddle. Now Waite barged forward.

"Where'd yuh run onto that hombre, chief?" he demanded.

"Why? What're you so interested about?" Holliday asked coldly. Chet felt a surge of hope.

"Well, I—I—run onto him afore," Waite said, a bit crestfallen. "An' I wasn't so damn' shore about him."

"He was with Biggers an' Fossum at the Shell creek shebang when yuh met that posse, wasn't he?" Holiday demanded.

"Yeah, he was. They vouched fer him, but it seemed tuh

me that he acted queer. He's either a damned rotten shot or he wasn't too anxious tuh help us."

"How come you three got away an' the other boys didn't?"

"That's easy," Waite said with a nervous laugh which he tried in vain to make sound natural. "I trusted this feller an' Fossum tuh hold one prong o' the ridge, an' they didn't do it. It looked like they was cut off, an' we'd all been caught if we'd stayed. Us three was smart enough tuh git away, so we grabbed the best horses an' flew."

Chet's hopes faded fast. Waite was lying atrociously, but more by accident than anything else his tale was corroborating the suspicions which Holliday already had.

"I see," Holliday stated. "If yuh knew that this hombre was a government detective it would explain why the sheriff's posse nearly got yuh, wouldn't it?"

"I'll say it would," Waite shouted. "Why, the dirty—" the outlaw poured out a string of filthy invective—"told us he was a friend o' yores. An' so did Fossum an' Biggers."

"Yeah, I know," Holliday said. "He had me fooled, too, for a little while. I told Jack an' Al tuh stay with him because I thought he was a cattle buyer an' we could git some good outa him."

"But I am a cattle buyer, an' I can prove it," Chet said quietly.

"That so?" Holliday queried with interest. "If so we'll give you a chance tuh prove it."

Chet felt that a pitfall yawned at his feet, but it was too neatly covered for him to see it.

"I told you I had a herd of cattle up here I wanted tuh sell," Holliday went on. "I'll give yuh a chance tuh buy 'em. You give me a draft for, say, twenty-five thousand dollars tuh pay for 'em, an' if it's honored yuh can go free as air."

The trap had been sprung. If he yielded, it would cost his employer twenty-five thousand dollars; if he refused, the outlaws would treat him as a spy.

THIRTEEN

THOUGH keenly aware of the precariousness of his postion Chet Kelvin didn't betray any trepidation by so much as the flicker of an eyelash.

"Deliver your cattle at Curryville and I'll give you the gold," he answered the outlaw leader's proposition coolly.

"That ain't the way we do business," Kirk Holliday replied. "We sell on the ground—an' take our money on the ground.

Too much danger of outlaws gettin' away with 'em if we tried tuh trail out." His followers burst into a guffaw of laughter.

"Then I'm afraid we can't do business." Chet shrugged.

"No?" Holliday's voice had become cold and menacing. "If that draft book in yore pocket is any good you'll make out that draft pronto so I can send a man out after the money. If yuh don't do it, or the draft ain't honored, I reckon there's trees grow high enough in this canyon tuh hang a man on. What about it?"

"Where are yore cattle?" Chet demanded, purposely obtuse.

"All around here. You seen some of 'em on the way in. If we git the money I'll guarantee the cattle will be here. I'll git yuh a bill o' sale for 'em from the rancher I got 'em from."

Chet began to comprehend the details of the scheme which Holliday had from the first intended to work upon him. The cattle were here all right, and they undoubtedly belonged to some rancher connected with the Wild Ones. They would be legitimately sold, but getting them out of this mountain fastness was something else again.

Somewhere along the trail, or even before, the Wild Ones would swoop down and stampede the cattle. That would be the end of the matter. It would cost more to gather them again than they were worth, and the same thing would happen if it were tried a second time. Eventually the man who had owned them would round them up and sell them again.

Deliberately to pay out twenty-five thousand dollars of his employer's money for no value at all was a proposition Chet wouldn't for a moment entertain. But he had been careful of his own money and had considerable saved up, enough to cover more than half of this amount.

"You can go to hell, Holliday," he said curtly. "It looks like we can't make a deal."

For a moment the baby-blue eyes of the tow-headed outlaw leader rested upon Chet, and there was in them a hint of admiration.

"Git down," he ordered. "It won't do you any good tuh try tuh git away because some of the boys will have their eyes on yuh all the time. Anything foolish yuh do will only make us have tuh tie yuh up."

"I thought we was gonna have a hangin' party," Chet challenged.

"Mebbe we will," the outlaw said levelly. "Don't git it into yore head that we ain't got the nerve. But I'm fair-minded, an' I'm givin' yuh a chance tuh back up that cattle buyin' bluff."

As Holliday dismounted, an outlaw stepped forward and handed the young chief a letter.

"Looks like this was from yore lawyer in Salt Lake," the outlaw said. "I got it when I come down from the north."

"Yes," Holliday said. For a second he studied the outside of the envelope, and Chet, with a single sweeping glance past the man's shoulder, made out the address on the envelope. It was: Mr. George B. Sullivan, Green Valley, Utah.

Holliday ripped the envelope open and silently read the letter. His followers watched his face with keen interest.

"H-m," he muttered. "This is damn' funny."

"What's in it, Kirk?" a man asked eagerly.

Apparently Holliday had few secrets from his followers, and he obviously wasn't a reticent man by nature, though he assuredly knew how to hold his tongue when necessary.

"You fellers all know Dude Johnson," he said.

The mention of that name was enough to cause Chet to prick up his ears. He had already learned from Jack Fossum that the man who went by that name was very probably the brother of Leda and Bud Harrison. The past few hours had been so full of surprising happenings that Chet had had little time to think about the affairs of the young Harrisons, but he hadn't forgotten them. He pretended to be busy with the little roan, but his ears were alert.

"Sure, we know him," an outlaw said. "Bobo there orta know him better'n anybody—him bein' the only one in that Soldier Summit job that got caught."

"Bobo seems tuh be developin' the habit o' gittin' away an' lettin' somebody else be caught," Blackie Payne spoke up drily.

"It was his own fault," Waite said angrily. "Had he used his head an' done what I said old man Wendall wouldn't 'a' caught him."

"Well, he's out," Holliday informed them.

"Why, I thought they give him twenty years—an' he's only been in a little over a year," the Peace River Kid blurted.

"It does seem funny," Holliday said. "So funny that Judge Barkwell thought it worth writin' about. I hired him tuh defend Dude, an' he's supposed tuh be lookin' out for any of the boys that gits snagged. But he says Dude has been released, an' he wasn't even notified that there was tuh be a hearin' by the pardon board."

"That seems funny," a man drawled. "That pardon board ain't usually so cussed keen about lettin' a Wild One go, once they git him in their clutches."

"How long's he been out, Kirk?" Bobo Waite asked.

"About three weeks."

"Funny, he ain't showed up, ain't it?"

"Maybe he's had a bellyful," Holliday said shortly. "I happen tuh know he come from good folks back East. He probably convinced the pardon board that if they'd let him out he'd go straight. No doubt his folks greased the way tuh git him out, an' he's gone home with 'em. If he has I don't blame him a damn' bit."

It was a strange speech from the leader of a gang of outlaws, but it showed that in his heart even Kirk Holliday wasn't altogether satisfied with the life he had chosen to lead. It showed that he had two sides to his nature, and it was perhaps this very fact that had made him undisputed leader.

The matter of Dude Johnson appeared to have been dismissed, but Chet couldn't dismiss it from his mind. He knew that if the man really was Charley Harrison, then it wasn't his folks who had got him out of the penitentiary. What had happened to him Chet neither knew nor cared, but it made him more than ever desirous of somehow reaching the I X L ranch to find out what sort of treatment his young friends had received.

That brought up the question of escape. Surrounded by twenty outlaws, that was seemingly impossible. And he knew that Kirk Holliday's talk about hanging was no idle threat. These men risked that fate every day of their lives, and it wouldn't seem in any way unusual that they should mete it out to an enemy—and Chet now knew entirely too much.

There seemed to be just one way in which he could escape the threatened hideous fate. That was to reconsider his refusal to give Holliday a draft for twenty-five thousand dollars. When the draft was found to be good they would know that he wasn't a detective who had been put upon their trail, and in due time he would probably be given his release. But it went against the grain to have to buy his own life—especially with other people's money.

On the other hand, he had no doubt whatever that the people he worked for would understand. They wouldn't approve of the way he had got himself into the scrape in the first place, but they would heartily urge him, if they knew, to buy his freedom. And he could pay them back eventually, even if it was, in the vernacular, "paying for a dead horse."

For the present, however, he was content to stall for time.

Dinner was soon ready, and the outlaws, after filling their plates and cups with steaming food and hot coffee, hunkered down wherever they could find any shade to eat. They were apparently a carefree, happy-go-lucky crew.

Chet helped himself to the tin hardware and took his turn at the mess box. He made it a point to seat himself as close to Holliday as possible. He observed that Bobo Waite had seated himself next to the leader.

"If yuh don't mind talkin' business, chief, where that lousy detective kin hear," Waite said, "just why did yuh send for us?"

Holliday gave a start. "What?" he blurted. "Who said I sent for yuh?"

"Wh-why, the word come from Bill Codd that you wanted tuh see us. We was on our way when we bumped into that damned sheriff an' his posse. The word was that if you wasn't at the I X L we was tuh come on over."

"Just how did yuh git that word?" Holliday said. "I reckon there ain't no danger of us sayin' anything that our friend here don't know."

"Well, yuh know we been hangin' out down at—well, out in the desert, an' been keepin' in touch with Codd," Waite began. "George Tandy rode down with the message which said you wanted us. Adam Broome had rode into Highriver an' told Codd that the message had been given tuh him by a stranger, but a feller who knew the password."

"A stranger, huh?" Holliday gritted. "Looks like old Jay Wendall was splashin' war medicine all over. If he ain't careful he'll git a dose of it down his own throat."

Everything Chet heard linked the I X L ranch closer and closer with the Wild Ones, and in consequence it brought the Harrisons more and more into danger.

"Then yuh never sent fer us?" Waite queried.

"No; I ain't got no use for yuh," Holliday said. Was it imagination, Chet wondered, or had there been a double meaning in the leader's tone?

"Then somebody double-crossed us an' dang near landed us in the pen," Waite said bitterly. "I knowed the minute I set eyes on this skunk here that he was a detective, but Jack Fossum was so shore of him I didn't do nothin'."

"Waite, yo're a liar an' a horsethief," Chet remarked evenly.

The big outlaw dropped his plate and his hand sought his gun. "By Gawd, I'll—" he rumbled.

"Drop it," Holliday snapped. "I'll tend tuh Kelvin's case." Waite, with a show of reluctance, picked up his plate.

For a few minutes Holliday was silent. "I'm beginin' tuh see light," he murmured presently, but he didn't say what light he was beginning to see.

"I reckon I kin too," Waite said. "This feller here has been sneakin' around, an' he's bribed somebody tuh double-cross us, or else that damned Dude Johnson has give him the low-down so he could pass himself off as one of us."

"Yuh may be right at that, Bobo," Holliday acknowledged.

"I reckon I'll take a little pasear over Highriver way myself an' see how things are stackin' up."

"What about us? Hadn't we better go back an' lay low for a while?" Waite asked.

"Yeah, I reckon yuh might as well," Holliday said.

"But we'd like tuh wait till this hombre gits his neck stretched," Waite said, with a jerk of his thumb toward Chet.

"You got a damn' queer appetite, Waite," Holliday said. "I'm leavin' because I don't like the looks o' such things. It's necessary sometimes, but I don't see how anybody can git any pleasure out of it."

"It'll be a pleasure tuh me." Waite grinned.

"Me too," Tony Mex chimed in with a laugh. "Maybe if I see this I'll know how tuh act if I ever have tuh go back to Arizona."

Holliday tossed his empty dishes toward the washtub in which the dishes were washed, and got to his feet.

"Well, what about it, Kelvin?" he asked. "If yo're a spy we've gotta deal with you. If yo're not yuh'd better be provin' it."

"I guess you've got me, Holliday," Chet sighed. "Most of what yo're talkin' is Latin tuh me, but I suppose you've got some reason tuh think as you do, an' a man don't lay down his life easily. I'm a cattle buyer an' nothin' else but. Give me some assurance that I'll be released when you git the money an' I'll make out that draft."

"If that draft turns out tuh be worth twenty-five thousand dollars in gold I'll know damn' well yo're no detective," Holliday said with a faint smile. "If the money comes back you'll be taken down near the Colorado line an' turned loose. It'll take yuh a week anyway tuh git back tuh civilization. By that time we'll be in Wyoming, but it'd pay yuh not tuh talk too much anyway. I got kind of a long arm."

"There's one condition before I pay you the money," Chet declared. "I've got two horses here—the glass-eyed gray that Tony there stole, an' the roan. I've got tuh have those two horses."

He saw a scowl settle over the dark features of Tony Mex as the fellow looked at Holliday anxiously.

"Generally the best claim a man can make tuh a horse around here is the ability tuh put his saddle on him." Holliday laughed. "The roan is yores. But if Tony wants tuh lay claim tuh the gray, he kin stick around here an' try tuh stop you from takin' him when yuh leave—if yuh ever do."

"Fair enough," Chet said curtly. "All I ask is an even break with him."

"You'll git yore gun then for the time bein'—if Tony chooses tuh keep his," Holliday decided.

There was a stormy, wrathful look on the Arizona murderer's face. An animal like the Mike horse wasn't picked up every day, and it was evident the fellow had set his heart upon keeping him. But Chet was just as stubborn.

Tony Mex wouldn't dare disobey Holliday's orders. It was apparent the man and his two companions weren't especially well liked by Holliday and the others. If Tony wanted the horse, he would have to fight for it. It would be excitement for the others, and quite probably Holliday rather hoped it would save him a lot of trouble if Tony succeeded in killing the cattle buyer.

"I'll stay—just in case this fellow should produce the gold —but the glass-eyed horse is mine, and I intend to keep him," Tony Mex said slurringly, as he got up and walked away.

Having decided to take the chance, Chet took out his draft book and made out an order, payable, as instructed by Holliday, to "Henry Stevens." The name was obviously one of Holliday's numerous aliases.

As soon as he had the draft Holliday called aside a young outlaw whom Chet had heard addressed as "Hurricane," and after talking with him a few minutes, handed him the draft. The outlaw put it in his pocket, saddled a horse and rode away.

"In four days Hurricane will be back, either with the gold or with proof that you're a liar," Holliday said coldly. "In the meantime don't try gittin' away. These men have orders tuh shoot the minute they see yuh git a hundred feet from camp."

At that moment Chet glanced up and caught a peculiar glance upon the face of Tony Mex. He realized that his chances to live out those four days were exceedingly small unless he kept a careful eye upon Tony Mex and his two associates. And now that he had given up the draft perhaps that was what Kirk Holliday secretly hoped for.

FOURTEEN

A BADLY worried man was Adam Broome. For twenty years he had been used as a tool by the boar-faced ruler of Highriver. Adam's intentions were good; had always been good. He wanted to do the right thing, but he was no Ajax to defy the lightning. His trouble now was that he didn't know from which way the lightning might strike hardest—from Bill Codd or the widow Gemmell.

For the immediate present he meant to follow the line he had always followed, that of least resistance.

As he left Mrs. Gemmell's house he encountered Nevada. He paused and extended his hand.

"Why, I know you," he said. "I thought yuh looked famil'ar when yuh passed in front o' the saloon. Yo're ole Nevader, who trapped in this country years ago. Caught more varmints than airy two trappers I ever saw since."

Nevada took the proffered hand. He was highly pleased by the flattery.

"Yeah, I've trapped Highriver from end tuh end," he admitted. "Yore face seems famil'ar, but—"

"Why, I'm Adam Broome, the owner o' the I X L ranch."

"Oh, shore," Nevada said, enlightened. "Yo're the feller we're lookin' for. We, er, that is, this gal I brung here she sorter seems tuh think—" Nevada stammered, and finally bogged down completely.

"Yeah, I know," Adam said. "She thinks a brother o' hers owns the I X L. She's a heap mistaken, but I shore don't wanta hurt a nice gal's feelin's. I'd a'most ruther give her the dinged ranch."

"Now that's whut I call bein' plumb generous," Nevada grinned. "I bet she'd be willin' tuh let yuh do chores around the place fer yore board if yuh done that."

"Come on over an' have a li'l drink," Adam invited as he linked his arm through that of the trapper. "We'd orta git together."

Nothing loath, Nevada paraded over to the saloon with his new-found friend.

They entered the saloon, and fat Bill Codd lumbered forward to meet them.

"This is ole Nevader who uster trap Highriver, Bill," Adam said. "You orter remember him."

"Shore I remember him," Codd said, and extended a fat and flabby hand. "Have a drink."

Bill Codd, however, had little time for the ex-trapper. "Excuse us," he grunted to Nevada, "we've got some business tuh talk over."

The saloonkeeper led the way to his private office, and wheeled upon his henchman. "Well?" he demanded.

"I didn't find out nothin' much," Adam squirmed, "except that that gal thinks some brother of hers owns the I X L. Nancy over there, she wants that I take 'em in an' pretend that mebbe the feller *did* sorta—"

"Did you tell her it was impossible?"

"Not eggzackly. Yuh see, Nance is still a heap suspicious that mebbe you an' me killed Martin. An' she's got more evidence agin me than I'd thought, so I—"

"Look here: have you been spillin' anything?" Codd ground out furiously.

"No, no—not a thing."

"You remember this, Broome: Any time anything breaks you'll hang for killin' Gemmell. You took him on the range that day, an' that bloodstained letter in his handwritin' is the same as a rope around your neck. I'm glad I didn't kill him instantly. He lived long enough tuh make you useful to me as long as you live."

"Yuh never told me before that it was you killed Martin," the rancher jerked out.

"If you hadn't been a fool yuh'd have known it. What difference does it make? The evidence is all against you," Codd sneered. "Now you'll do what I say about that gal, an' not what Nance Gemmell tells yuh."

"O' course, o' course," Adam said hastily. "But I figgered thisaway: I'll let 'em go out there, but I'll git on the good side o' this here Nevader an' explain tuh him that I jest don't wanta hurt their feelin's. Then I'll give him a hint tuh let 'em know I'm jest bein' kind an' fatherly, an' when they ask fer the truth I'll jest be obleeged tuh tell 'em. That'll git rid of 'em, an' no harm done."

"Maybe," Codd frowned. "But there's more back of this than some fool outlaw's big talk. Jay Wendall an' Nance Gemmell have been after my scalp for years, an' I think this is all a scheme of theirs. All right. You let 'em go out there. I'll find out what's back of it, an' if I can't make some use of them young people then Bill Codd is losin' his grip."

It was the next morning before Nevada learned from his employer that Adam Broome had practically conceded their claim to his ranch.

"We'll go right out there at once, please," Leda said when she had finished her explanation. "My brother does own the I X L ranch and he's certain to return before long. We'll go out there and wait."

" 'Scuse me, miss, but who was it told yuh about yore brother ownin' it?" Nevada asked.

"Why, Mr. Broome himself, the very man that that Bishop Carey said was an outlaw, admitted it to Mrs. Gemmell."

Nevada fidgeted with the bellyband of a horse he was harnessing, but said nothing. He knew there was a bug under the chip some place, but how to reveal it to the girl in a way that he would be believed was beyond his powers.

Mrs. Gemmell came out to the buckboard to see them off.

The woman's life had been a lonely one, and now she felt an almost overwhelming desire to mother these two young waifs from the East. Their colossal ignorance of what they were going to face had at once aroused her pity and her strong protective instincts. After a life spent on the frontier Nancy Gemmell was as able to face its problems as any man.

"You'll find it lonesome out there," she told them. "You just go out and look around, an' then come back here. It won't cost yuh a cent."

"You're awfully kind," Leda said gratefully. "But if Charley is in some kind of trouble I think it is our duty to stay there and do what we can."

"An' I've always wanted to live on a ranch," Bud said. "I don't see anything very excitin' around here," he added with disapproving frankness.

"You take care of 'em," Mrs. Gemmell adjured Nevada as they drove away.

It was a rough, lonely road they followed as it twisted its way around the base of a flock of barren hills; gleaming with magnificent coloring after an early morning shower. Eroded to strange and spectacular shapes, these hills thrust themselves skyward in colors ranging from blood-red to pink. They were gashed by deep, precipitous gullies washed out by the rushing waters of untold thousands of violent storms.

It was a wild, eerie, awe-inspiring country—the acme of lonesomeness. Ever the buckboard moved slowly upward, and Leda Harrison's soul seemed to shrivel into nothingness through a sense of being such an atom in this land of vast and rugged distances. At first she had chattered gaily with Bud and the guide, but presently she was keeping a depressed silence.

Why, she asked herself, had Charley ever come to such a place? What could it possibly offer to one who loved life, and the comforts of life as he did? He had not come there willingly, on that she would have staked her life.

She consoled herself with the thought that within a few hours she would have a talk with this Adam Broome and find out the true state of affairs.

It was almost noon before the country began to open up. The first break in the monotony of too gorgeously colored hills was a long, low mesa, or plain, covered with pines. Beyond them she quickly got glimpses of higher and more broken mountains, their slopes heavily timbered up to gray timber line.

Then the country suddenly opened up into a small valley. From behind the end of the pine-clad mesa came a spur, and in this triangular flat lay the hay meadows of the I X L. The ranch buildings, once well-kept and pretentious, were just visible against a background of brush-covered hillside. Even at that distance the girl could see the sagging roof of a great barn, and the paint on the house was no more than a reminiscence.

"That orta be the best ranch in the state," Nevada declared. "That crick that comes a-tearin' in from the other side of the mesa has just water enough fer this place an' no more. That gives the I X L a strangleholt on that range between there an' timber line, tuh say nothin' o' this here main valley that runs back up yon way fer twenty-five miles an' is fine fer winter grazin'."

"It—it must be a big proposition," Leda faltered. She was accustomed to the small farms of the East and was simply unable to grasp the tremendous scope of all that lay before her; all of which, she had been led to believe, belonged to her brother.

"Could run ten thousand head o' cattle easy as nothin'," old Nevada assured her.

The remainder of their way lay across a level sagebrush flat. On their way they saw two cowpunchers swing in ahead of them hazing a bunch of wild range horses into the corrals. Bud wriggled with excitement.

As they drove up into a hard-packed open place below the house and above the outbuildings, they saw five or six men roosting upon the top poles of the corral that held the snorting band of range horses. The men turned their brown, leathery faces toward the buckboard with undisguised curiosity, and Leda's heart became a leaden little lump in her bosom. Her small, firm fingers were clasped so tight that they were bloodless.

She saw a tall, gangling fellow with an ugly face just visible beneath the wide and flopping brim of an immense hat shuffling loose-jointedly toward her. The man raised a dangling arm in a careless salute.

"Howdy, folks, howdy," the man greeted. "We been 'xpectin' yuh. Had the greaser cleanin' up all mornin' long. 'H'ain't much useter entertainin' ladies, but we hope yuh'll be comfortable, miss."

"Thank you—I'm sure I will," Leda said hurriedly. "You—are Mr. Broome?"

"Yep, I'm Adam Broome."

Leda leaned forward eagerly. "Tell me about my brother," she begged. "How long has he been away? When will he be back?"

"Wall, now, Miss Harrison, that's a long story," Adam evaded.

"But surely you can tell me how long since he left."

"Wal, he ain't been around here fer nearly a year, tuh tell the truth."

"A year?"

"It's thisaway, ma'am: I sold the I X L tuh Charley on jaw-bone mostly. He was shore he could raise the money in the East tuh pay fer it, but I reckon his friends musta kinda turned him down. Final, he told me tuh take an' run it till he raised the money. If he gits it I reckon he'll come back. If he can't he won't," Adam stated.

"That isn't the way he talked or wrote," Leda couldn't help saying.

She got down and followed Broome up to the front door of the ranch house. A grinning old Mexican, spotlessly clean, but wrinkled as an old boot, met them at the door.

"Show these young people where they'll live, Fernando, an' do everything yuh kin tuh make 'em comf'table an' happy," Adam said hurriedly, and beat an immediate retreat.

"Coom right in." Old Fernando bowed. "Iss pleasoor to mak' you 'appy. Anyt'ing you want you please to tell ole Fernando."

"Thank you," Leda said. She followed the old man toward the room he had prepared for her, and found that it was scrupulously clean.

Fernando was palpably anxious to win her approval. He showed her the kitchen and she was pleased to find it as clean as the rest of the house. Savory dishes were cooking on the stove. She made the old man happy by unstinted praise.

"Eet is long tam since be señora or señorita on dees plaze," he said. "Mus' be twent' year since Señora Gemmell she 'ave gone away. Mebbe Fernando he no savvy w'at young señorita lak', but 'e try for feex."

"You have been here ever since Mrs. Gemmell left the I X L?" Leda queried eagerly. "Then you must have known my brother well. Tell me about him."

Old Fernando plainly showed his distress. "Your broth' 'e not show up 'ere ver' mooch, but 'e damn fine caballero all same," he declared. "Caramba! Dat chicken she burn."

The old man flew to his oven and busied himself frantically basting a fowl which Leda was housewife enough to know didn't need attention. She returned slowly to her room.

The dark mystery surrounding her brother was deepening with every hour. None of these people were willing even to talk about him. That strengthened her belief that Charley had met with foul play, but if so, and these people had stolen his ranch, why had they raised no objections to the presence of her and Bud?

Then a cold, stark feeling of fear shot through her mind. Was it possible that these outlaws planned to eliminate her and Bud as she feared they had Charley? In something of a panic she called to Bud, but he wasn't in his room.

Stepping over to the window she saw her brother down at the corrals, mingling with the cowhands. He was obviously having the time of his life.

FIFTEEN

CHET's surmise that Kirk Holliday really hoped that Tony Mex would obviate the necessity for hanging him, or turning him loose according to the agreement, was strengthened next morning when the outlaw leader rode away with his chief lieutenant, Blackie Payne. Over half the outlaw crew had been sent out somewhere, but the three in whom Chet was most interested remained. And no effort had been made to restrict his movements, save that terse verbal warning not to get more than a hundred feet from the camp.

All through the day he could see Bobo Waite, Tony Mex, and the Peace River Kid whispering among themselves, but he was careful not to give them any excuse to exercise their treachery.

At the same time he was constantly upon the alert to seize any chance that might offer to effect his escape. He had kissed the twenty-five thousand goodbye when he wrote out the draft; so there was nothing to be gained by staying there if he should get a chance to get away. But there never was a time when his movements weren't being watched.

He felt that he had just one chance. The day before he had seen Blackie Payne go into a small tent which was reserved for him and Holliday. When the man entered the handle of Chet's sixgun had been protruding from the top of a chaps pocket. When he came out the gun was missing. And when the two men rode away that morning there had been no sign of the gun. Blackie carried two guns anyway, and he wasn't likely to burden himself with a third and unnecessary weapon. Chet was convinced that the gun was in that tent. If he could once get inside and make a search—

The opportunity was slow in coming. There were always eyes upon him in the daytime, and at night he was compelled to sleep between two of his captors, with others lying all about.

Nothing of any interest happened all that day, and Chet suffered from boredom. The only man he found willing to talk at all was the cook, a middle-aged fellow with a wooden leg, who was disposed to be friendly, despite a most ferocious-looking red mustache.

The outlaws were lazy, and none of them would help the cook.

To pass the time Chet volunteered his services and the offer was accepted gladly.

The second morning of his stay at the outlaw camp they had hot cakes for breakfast. While "Speck," the cook, was busy with his batter and a long griddle Chet stood by ready to lend a hand. The meal was half over, and the outlaws were clamoring for hot ones, when Speck discovered that his water bucket was empty.

"Go git me a bucket o' water, will ye, lad?" he requested Chet.

The latter picked up the bucket and looked toward the creek.

"Has anybody here got any doubt about the creek bein' less than a hundred feet away?" he demanded.

"That's all right," said an outlaw called "Sonora" Yates, "but remember that it ain't necessary tuh cross the creek tuh fill yore bucket. If yuh do yuh might slip."

"Keep an eye on me," Chet invited, as he started away.

The place where he would fill his bucket was in plain view of where the outlaws were eating, but to reach it he had to pass back of the tent where most of them slept, and here he was out of sight of all but Speck. And right behind that tent was the one which Holliday and Payne occupied.

It wasn't by accident that that pail had become empty. Chet had seen to that when Speck's back was turned. And at about the same time he contrived to slip a butcher knife under the waistband of his pants.

He went straight to the creek and filled the water bucket. He knew that alert eyes were upon him, watching for him to make a false move. With the appearance of having all the leisure in the world at his disposal he turned and sauntered back toward the camp.

The moment he got between the two tents he became a dynamo of action. He was out of sight of all the men except the cook, and Speck's back was toward him. He dropped the bucket and with a single stroke of the butcher knife cut the fastenings of the tent flap. He didn't dare take the time to untie them. In a second he was inside, his eyes searching for the most likely place for the gun to be.

His eyes lighted at once upon a pair of warbags. He leaped upon them and felt frantically for a telltale bulge. He quickly found it. In a flash he had got possession of his own six-gun. What to do with it was still a question.

Any unusual bulge about his person would surely attract the vigilant gaze of the outlaws. It was still early enough in the morning, for all that the indolent outlaws were late risers, to justify a coat. For the present Chet slipped the gun inside his shirt, and shoved it around to where it would be concealed by the fall of his coat. As soon as possible he hoped to ditch the weapon somewhere till the time of need.

He pulled the tent flaps together as best he could, and they hung straight down. Unless a wind happened to come up and stir them they weren't likely to be noticed. Picking up the water bucket he strolled up to the fire.

Immediately after breakfast two men mounted their night horses and rode out to get the cavvy. Chet observed another furtive whispering among his three pet animosities. Something, he was sure, was in the wind. He changed his mind about wanting to ditch the gun.

By the time he and Speck had eaten their breakfasts the cavvy had been corralled inside the long ropes which, stretched around a group of trees, formed a serviceable corral. His eyes at once picked out his own two animals. There was a lot of aimless banter, and a few bucking expositions which consumed considerable time; but finally only seven men were left at the camp. Among them were the three train robbers. But of these three Tony Mex seemed disposed to take a ride. Moreover, he was going to do it on the Mike horse. Chet's face began to harden.

A minute later it grew harder still. With unnecessary brutality the fellow kicked the inoffensive gray in the ribs. Then, as the surprised animal bounded aside, Tony doubled up the end of his lasso rope and brought it down across the horse's ears with a terrific thump. It was uncalled for, and senselessly brutal. Chet knew how terribly painful such punishment must be. But Tony Mex didn't stop. He continued his attack muttering furious oaths, and the horse, though it kicked and plunged inside the corral, was powerless to get away.

The shameful cruelty of the thing made Chet Kelvin see red. But he didn't lose his head. He recognized instantly that this was the culmination of the plot his foes had been whispering about. The corral was about three hundred feet from the camp. The men had figured that he would run down there to make a protest. And before he got half way there he would have crossed the fatal deadline and they could shoot him down with impunity.

He wasn't to be tricked into such a trap. On the other hand, he wasn't minded to stand idly by and watch his pet horse being abused.

For a moment he pretended not to see, though he knew that the others were watching him curiously. He had turned his back, and he seized the opportunity to tear open his shirt and get his hand on the grips of his gun. Then, just as he was about to whirl back, he received unexpected support.

"By Gawd, that kind o' thing is onnecessary, an' it burns me

84

up," roared Speck. "I'm gonna stop that if you fellers don't. I never liked that greaser-lookin' galoot nohow."

"Aw, close your face, yuh peg-legged pot wrastler," the Peace River Kid snarled.

"No cheap tinhorn train robber kin talk tuh me like that," Speck howled angrily, and reached for a stick of wood.

The Peace River Kid drew his gun. He saw no necessity for a fast draw, and he drew with cold deliberation. For the moment the eyes of the other outlaws were upon him and Speck. As Speck straightened up with the club the Peace River Kid leveled his gun. But he didn't have a chance to show whether he meant to shoot or was only bluffing.

There came the report of a gun; with a cry of mingled pain and rage the Peace River Kid held up a broken and mangled hand. His gun fell into the dirt.

The other five outlaws whirled as one man, and the hands of all but Speck slapped gunward. But their amazed glances fell upon the smoking weapon in Chet Kelvin's hand, and at his crisp word of command their hands jerked back.

"Line up an' look purty," Chet snapped. "Unbuckle yore gun belts an' back away from 'em." His tone warned them that he meant business. Not one of them cared to risk death by failing to obey. Speck alone did not move.

Chet was placed where the men were between him and Tony Mex. At the report of the gun the outlaw had desisted from his belaboring of the now frantic horse, and after a single swift glance of comprehension he had gone for his gun. But he dared not fire at Chet because of the almost dead certainty that he would hit one of his friends. His plain course, therefore, was to make a run for the brush and get at the prisoner from behind.

Dropping the rope, the man started for the nearest timber. As he did so he passed behind the Mike horse. Already the frenzied horse had kicked out blindly several times while the outlaw was fighting him. Now, suspecting some new torture, the wild-eyed animal doubled up quickly and lashed out with both feet. Tony Mex was at just the right distance to receive the full shock of both ironshod hoofs right between the shoulders. He hit the ground so hard that he skidded, and he didn't get up.

This was a break Chet hadn't expected, but he was quick to take advantage of it.

"I'm goin' away from here, hombres," he told the outlaws evenly, "an' it ain't gonna be healthy for anybody tuh git in my way. Speck's the only halfway decent one among yuh, so I'm gonna let him tie the rest of you up. Fly at it, Speck, an' if yuh linger too much on the knots or don't make 'em tight enough

I'll comb your bald pate with a gun barrel as quick as I would any of the others."

"You tie me up, an' I'll git yuh fer it," Bobo Waite roared at the cook. "Hadn't been fer you chippin' in he wouldn't uh got the drop on us."

"Yah! Threaten me, will yuh?" Speck roared angrily. "This whole thing was a frame-up tuh git this feller killed so's yuh could excuse yoreselves tuh Kirk. Tuh show yuh how much I'm afraid o' you, Waite, I'll tie yuh so dang tight yore guts'll ache."

Chet smiled grimly. While he kept the outlaws covered, Speck went to work with a right good will with a convenient cotton bed-rope.

By the time Speck had Bobo Waite and the Peace River Kid tied up his ardor had lagged but, prodded by Chet, he trussed up the other three. The whole performance had taken not over twenty minutes.

Without hesitation Chet tied Speck's hands behind his back but otherwise allowed him liberty of movement. Then he went to the corral and caught Mike and the roan pacer. Tony Mex was still lying very still. Chet ascertained that the fellow was still breathing, but there was little danger of him taking any considerable interest in things for quite a while.

Leading the two horses up to the tents, Chet threw his saddle upon Mike, and then packed a bed-roll and some grub on the little roan. He confiscated a rifle from an outlaw's saddle, and was ready to travel.

His last act before leaving camp was to turn loose every horse. Even if the men got loose they would be afoot until some of their pals arrived and drove in the horses. None of them were likely to return before noon.

He was well out of a tight situation. Had he remained it was almost certain that Tony Mex and his pals would have contrived to murder him. But he knew that he would be out twenty-five thousand dollars, and whatever of leniency there had been in his attitude toward the Wild Ones was a thing of the past.

In a word, a state of war existed between him and them. He meant to get in touch with Sheriff Jay Wendall at the earliest opportunity and offer that fighting officer his services.

But his first business was to get away from the vicinity of Stag-tail butte as rapidly as possible. He knew that the hills were full of outlaws, and at any moment he might encounter some of them. To avoid that danger it seemed necessary to hide out in some likely place until dark. But if he did that he would be that much closer to the outlaw camp when the alarm was raised, and that would happen not later than noon.

His first destination was the town of Highriver. There he

hoped to find out something about the I X L ranch. In view of the fact that Kirk Holliday and Blackie Payne had apparently headed for that place, he knew that it would be extremely unwise to barge in there, alone and unannounced.

He knew the general direction he wanted to go, and though constantly looking for a safe place to halt he found none that suited him, and kept on going. Once he was away from the immediate locality of Stag-tail butte he had little fear of being overtaken. His concern was to make sure that he didn't meet anybody unexpectedly.

That night he slept in a copse with his two horses staked where he could hear if anything disturbed them. But he didn't build a fire. The next morning, after reconnoitering carefully he built a fire and cooked breakfast. He was soon on his way.

A couple of hours' riding brought him to a plainly marked trail. Thus far he had been merely traveling across country. The trail was running the way he wanted to go, but he was hesitant about traveling it. There was considerable pine timber in the canyon down which the trail wandered, and he might unexpectedly bump into some of the Wild Ones coming up the other way. On the other hand, it was rough going in any other direction.

Eventually he decided to try the trail, but he kept every sense alert.

It was an hour or so later that he distinctly heard the sound of voices a short distance ahead of him. He checked his horses instantly, and gazed about. There was no place of concealment that he could possibly reach before whoever it was came in sight.

Just below him grew a clump of four or five twisted pine trees, and the trail evidently made a bend just below them. In a second he was out of the saddle; he quit the trail and ran rapidly along the side-hill the short distance to the trees. Now he could distinctly hear the fall of every horse's foot, and the creaking of saddles. One of the men approaching was whistling a tune.

Chet leaned his weight against the bole of a gnarled pine, and thumbed the hammer of his gun. The men would appear in sight not more than twenty feet from him. At the same instant they would see his horses. But he didn't believe they would see him until he had them covered with his gun, and he was in no mood for a return journey to Stag-tail butte.

SIXTEEN

CHET had just time to note the bobbing peaks of three cowboys hats before the riders came into view. Owing to the bend of the trail and a thick sarvis bush, he saw the men's backs before he did their faces. He saw the man on lead jerk his horse to an abrupt halt and heard him utter an ejaculation of surprise as he saw the gray and the roan.

"Git 'em up!" Chet snapped in a voice which spelled business.

Three pairs of hands went automatically skyward. Three surprised faces twisted around in his direction, and then it was Chet's turn to get a surprise.

"Well, I'll be damned!" he ejaculated.

Two of the three men were Al Biggers and Jack Fossum! The third man was a stranger to Chet. Chet's first question under the circumstances was quite a natural one.

"Where's Brandy Waters?" he demanded. If the men had broken jail and the vicious young Waters was to be expected along soon he wanted to know it.

A friendly grin spread over Jack Fossum's face. "He's back in jail—I'm happy tuh say," he said. "Hello, Chet. What yuh gonna do with that cannon?"

"Shoot the ears off the first hombre that moves," Chet declared frostily. But he was feeling the charm of Jack Fossum's likable personality and was already aware that there would be no shooting so far as Jack was concerned.

"What's the big idee stickin' us up again?" Al Biggers rasped angrily. "You a John Law or somethin'?"

"I expect tuh be soon, Biggers, an' if I was now I'd shore be takin' you back in with me. Mebbe I will anyway. How come you got outa jail?"

"Do we have tuh do all that talkin' with our hands up?" Fossum asked mildly.

"If there's no monkey business you can take 'em down. But don't any of you go tuh playin' with yore shootin' irons. An' I'll be keepin' mine handy."

"Hear that, boys?" Fossum remarked. "Doctor's orders. Take it with a smile. We shore don't wanta git nothin' worse."

Until now Chet had paid little attention to the third man, except to make sure that he didn't act foolish about his gun. Now he regarded him more intently. He knew he could depend upon Jack keeping his word, and Jack would see that Biggers behaved. But this third man might be dangerous. He noticed

88

that the man was young and rather good-looking despite a sullen mouth and a stubborn chin. Then, suddenly, it struck him right between the eyes who this stranger was. Notwithstanding the disparity in age and size, this man, from the mouth up, bore a startling resemblance to Bud Harrison. Chet looked for the scar from eye to brow which Jack Fossum had once mentioned, and it was there.

This, then, was "Dude" Johnson, outlaw. Associate of Bobo Waite in the Soldier Summit train robbery. Brother of the girl for whose sake Chet had risked his life and lost his savings.

The three men had lowered their hands to their saddle forks, and were waiting for Chet to start the meeting.

"Do we open with prayer?" Jack drawled.

"It mightn't be a bad idea at that," Chet replied. "Who let you out of jail?"

Jack jerked his thumb toward Harrison. "Friend of ours there," he said. "Dude, I wantcha tuh meet Chet Kelvin. He's the cattle buyer who he'ped us fight off Wendall's posse the other day."

Harrison nodded coldly. Did the fellow know that his brother and sister were in the country? Chet wondered.

"Oh, yes," Chet remarked. "You told me something about Johnson one time, didn't you? Something about the I X L."

Fossum shot Chet a warning glance, and a look of keen, hard suspicion glinted in Harrison's eyes.

"Yeah, I believe I did," Jack answered. "I won't fool yuh, Chet. You see the sheriff let his posse go, an' sent us on with his two deputies. We didn't git tuh Newdale that first night, so we stopped at a ranch. It just happened that Dude here was hangin' around that ranch, so he waited for his chance an' when the deps got tuh sleep he slipped in an' got the drop on 'em. When he invited me an' Al tuh ride away with him we thought it wouldn't be polite tuh refuse."

"I see. An' why didn't yuh bring Brandy Waters along?"

"Simply because Brandy belonged tuh the Bobo Waite faction an' they hadn't treated Dude exactly right."

"I've been a kind of a prisoner, too. But I had tuh pretty much manage my own escape," Chet stated.

"The hell? What happened tuh you?"

"I fell in with yore friends, Hank Stevens an' Happy Mack," Chet said. "They got the idea that somebody had leaked tuh the sheriff about Waite's crew bein' on the way tuh keep an appointment with Kirk Holliday—which neither of 'em had ever made. At first they thought it was me, an' that I'd led you an' Al into the same trap. They're still convinced I'm a detective."

"Say, you musta been in a tough spot."

"I was, kinda," Chet grinned. "Waite was at Holliday's

camp when we got there, an' he done some first-class lyin'. Made Holliday believe I was responsible for you bein' trapped, an' that him an' his two pards couldn't do nothin' but git away."

"I'd like tuh been there when he was sayin' that," Biggers gritted.

"How'd yuh come tuh git away?" Jack asked.

Chet told them in a few words, not omitting to mention the draft he had given Holliday for twenty-five thousand dollars. He saw their eyes glitter when he related that part.

"Boy, I knowed you was good when yuh stuck me an' Al up that night," Jack laughed, "but I never knowed yuh was that good. Standin' up seven Wild Ones is one fer the books. If you wanta take me back tuh the calaboose I'll go along peaceable."

"I don't think I'll bother about takin' anybody in today," Chet said, "but I don't mind sayin' that now I've got acquainted with yore Wild Ones I don't care a whale of a lot about 'em."

"Aw, you just got tuh see their worst side," Jack laughed. "They're meek as lambs generally. But we'll see that Holliday is put straight about you. You leave it tuh us."

"What about the twenty-five thousand?" Chet demanded.

"It looks," Jack grinned again, "like yuh'd bought a bunch o' cattle."

"I thought so."

"Yuh say Hurricane went out tuh git the draft cashed, an' won't be back for a coupla more days? That'll give me time tuh work on Kirk an' see if I can't persuade him tuh ack reasonable."

"If yuh can find him. My understandin' was that him an' Payne had gone tuh the I X L."

"Mebbe so. I reckon you ain't hankerin' tuh meet 'em just now?"

"No."

"Then if I was you I'd take the right-hand fork when I got down here about three miles. It's a bit farther, but there's not much danger o' meetin' anybody unless it's a I X L puncher," Jack advised.

Chet was dying to ask Charley Harrison if he knew about Bud and Leda, but he didn't dare do it because of the fear that it might cause even worse complications for the girl and boy. The man himself was something of an enigma.

"I have an idea," Chet remarked pensively, "that the outfit over there may be a bit surprised tuh see yore friend."

For the first time Harrison opened his mouth, and he did it quickly. "What about me?" he shot out.

"Well, it seems that Holliday's lawyer, a Judge Barkwell, I believe, was so plumb flabbergasted at findin' you'd got out of the penitentiary that he took it on himself tuh write Holliday all about it. I happened tuh be there when Holliday read the letter."

Though Chet spoke casually, he was intently watching every play of the man's features. Though Harrison laughed, his laughter didn't ring true. And there was an undeniable flicker of fear in his eyes.

"Yes, he would be surprised," the man said cynically. "If I'd waited for him tuh git me out I'd have rotted there."

"I'd be just like yuh, Dude," Al Biggers burst out. "Tuh hell with monkeyin' with lawyers. I'd make a break fer it just like you did."

Harrison said nothing, though he cast a surreptitious glance at Chet. The latter was quick to see the discrepancy between the tale Harrison must have told and what the lawyer had written. It might be that Harrison was only a teller of tall tales. The letters he had written to his folks telling them of his ownership of the I X L indicated as much. But there might be more to it than that.

Bobo Waite and his men knew that somebody had tricked them into the hands of the sheriff, from whom they had narrowly escaped. If they found out that Harrison was in the country, they would certainly suspect him. Particularly so when they found out that he had been pardoned out of the penitentiary instead of escaping as he claimed.

And suddenly Chet wondered if Harrison hadn't done just that. It was unusual, to say the least, for him to be pardoned so quickly and for so grave an offense. And why had he been on the ground so conveniently to help Fossum and Biggers escape? They weren't the men Sheriff Wendall was after anyway. Had not the sheriff permitted Harrison to let them go for the purpose of causing the Wild Ones to trust Harrison, so that he could lead them into another trap?

The more he thought about it the more convinced he became that he had hit upon the truth. If Harrison went on the Stagtail butte his story would be punched full of holes by the outlaws, and he would undoubtedly meet the fate which had been decreed for Chet if he failed to prove that he wasn't a spy.

"I might as well tell yuh the rest," Chet went on with seeming carelessness. "Bobo Waite was plumb inclined tuh believe that you was the man who faked the message that Holliday wanted tuh see him an' the others. The reason Holliday didn't believe it was because he was plump imbued with the idea that I was back of it, an' besides he had it figgered that yore rich folks in the East had bought yuh outa the pen."

If Harrison didn't realize his immense danger from that, then he was dense indeed.

91

"Waite would say that," Harrison gritted. "The way he let you boys down wasn't nothing to the way he double-crossed me. But I'm not asking any sheriff to even up with him. I'll do that little job myself."

The words were brave enough, but the manner didn't ring true. If ever a man was frightened to the very core of his soul, Charles Harrison was that man.

Chet felt sorry for him. He glanced at Jack Fossum, and he read in the expression of that young man a faint tinge of contempt. Biggers alone took the words at their face value.

"Me an' Jack'll be right alongside tuh take Tony an' the Peace River Kid off yore hands," that worthy chirped.

"I'm not asking for any help," Harrison said. "All I want is to be sure that Holliday and the others keep hands off."

He turned to Chet. "Did you say Holliday left for the I X L?"

Chet nodded.

"I'll tell yuh what I'll do," Harrison said. "The man I want to see first is Kirk Holliday. I'll ride back down with this man an' show him where the trail forks off. Then I'll go on tuh the I X L and if I don't meet Kirk on the way I'll find him there."

"Aw, why go tuh that bother?" Al Biggers objected. "Le's have it out with the skunks right now."

"There's no use having the whole mob jump us," Harrison argued desperately. "With Kirk on our side we'll have 'em foul."

"Right," Jack Fossum said shortly. "I think that's the best way."

Chet had long since holstered his gun. Now he walked back to his horses and the others joined him there.

"Well, Chet," Jack Fossum said, as he reached out to shake hands, "when yuh git ready tuh come gunnin' for us send me a postal card, will yuh, so I can duck out of sight."

"I'll do my best, Jack," Chet promised. "Take care of yourself, and I may be seein' yuh. If I can ever do yuh any good let me know."

Fossum and his companion rode on up the trail. Chet stuck his toe into the stirrup and stepped up. He could see that Harrison was eager to hit the back trail. The moment Chet struck the saddle they started down the canyon.

Chet felt that he simply had to find out something more about the man. Harrison had undoubtedly been given a tremendous scare, and yet Chet had a feeling that he was no coward.

"I take it you an' me are purty much in the same boat," Chet ventured mildly. "We'd probably both stretch hemp if we fell into the hands of the Wild Ones."

Harrison looked back over his shoulder. "Just what do you mean?" he asked.

"You was let outa the pen so's yuh could help Sheriff Wendall nab the Bobo Waite gang, wasn't you?" Chet asked bluntly.

"You're right," Harrison answered after a minute of silence. "I am working for Wendall. And you undoubtedly saved my life by telling me about that letter from Barkwell. It wasn't supposed to get out that I'd been paroled. I'm grateful to you."

"That's all right," Chet said. "The question is: what're you goin' tuh do now?"

"Why do you want to know?" the man demanded bluntly.

Chet had been thinking things over. It would hurt Leda Harrison terribly to know that her brother was an outlaw and a liar, but even that might be better than continued uncertainty. And if the fellow could establish the fact that he had reformed and was trying to aid the law that would be a mighty factor in his favor. He had decided to tell.

"It's not very much to me personally," he said quietly, "but I know a girl and boy who might be a heap interested."

Harrison swung his horse to the side of the trail so that they might ride abreast.

"I don't quite follow you," he frowned.

"I think you will," Chet replied a bit curtly. "The other day when I was down in Curryville I run onto a young woman who with her kid brother was lookin' for another brother—one that they thought was the owner of the big I X L ranch. What happened to 'em I don't know, but they were still on their way when I saw 'em the last time at Boxtown. Their name was Harrison."

He knew that it was an abrupt, almost brutal way of breaking the news, but after all the man had it coming to him. Harrison had sowed thistles of deception; he couldn't expect to garner figs of joy. But the man was more shaken than Chet even expected. His complexion altered to an ashen gray. His whole body trembled.

"My God," he moaned.

SEVENTEEN

Leda had found nothing to complain of in her treatment at the I X L. Adam Broome, in his eccentric way, treated her with every deference, and old Fernando was almost servile in his desire to please. As for Bud, all the dreams of his young life were coming true. He was learning to ride, rope, and shoot.

But despite this the time passed slowly. The monotony was unbroken. She missed the society of her own kind, and above all nothing occurred to shed light upon the mystery of her brother's disappearance.

Once, indeed, old Nevada hinted that it was passing strange that no employee of the ranch had the faintest knowledge of Charley Harrison, and the old guide ventured the opinion that Adam Broome was a man with an uncommonly kind heart.

"Jest a sentimental ole idjit," Nevada opined. "Why, I wouldn't put it a-past him tuh keep you an' Buddy around here fer years ruther than hurt yore feelin's."

"You mean to say you don't believe Charley was ever on this ranch?" Leda demanded, half angrily.

"Wal, it seems funny—"

"It is funny—funny that none of these men care to talk about Charley," the girl said hotly. "None of them know anything about him, yet I've seen enough to know that Charley has been here a great deal. Why, he's described the whole place to us in detail, even to the number of rooms in this very house."

It was too much for Nevada, who beat a hasty retreat.

The incident only tended to strengthen the girl's fear that the place was a nest of lawbreakers, and that Charley had met with foul play. But rather than spoil Bud's fun she kept her suspicions of the I X L crew strictly to herself.

She had been at the ranch but a short while when something disturbed her more than ever. She saw a puncher gallop wildly into the place and excitedly convey some piece of information to Adam Broome. She could tell by the attitude of all hands that they were under a strain of some sort. A few of the men saddled up hurriedly and left the ranch. The rest acted queerly.

Half an hour later she saw a gray-mustached man ride quietly into the ranch on a bay horse. She could see nothing menacing about him, but she guessed that he was the cause of all the sudden activity. She saw the man apparently talking in a casual manner to Adam Broome, and finally he went over to the corral where Bud was playing with a young colt and engaged him in conversation.

At last the grizzled rider turned and walked toward the house. Broome started to accompany him, but at a word from the stranger turned back. It was then that Leda noticed the star on the man's vest.

When old Fernando opened the door she heard a gruff voice saying: "I want tuh talk tuh the young lady that's here. You tell her Sheriff Wendall would like a few words with her."

Leda didn't wait to be told. "Come right in here, sheriff, please," she said quietly, but for some reason her nerves were fluttering.

The gruff-voiced but kindly sheriff quickly put her at her ease.

"Please set down, Miss Harrison," he begged. "This is no

cross-examination, so yuh don't need have any fear of me. Yuh don't have tuh answer any question yuh don't want to."

"Thank you," she breathed. "I don't see any reason why I shouldn't answer any question you might ask."

"That's fine," the sheriff said. He paused for a moment while he took in the girl's trim, slender beauty. There was keen appraisal in his gray eyes, and Leda Harrison passed muster. Sheriff Wendall had daughters of his own.

"I had a little talk with yore kid brother a while ago," he said mildly. "You an' him have come a long ways. I hope you ain't gonna be disappointed in what you come for."

"What do you mean, sheriff?" Leda asked quickly.

"Well, about this ranch here, for instance. If your brother don't show up, have you got any papers to show yore rights?"

"Only a letter from him," Leda acknowledged. "I suppose it won't be enough. But if my brother has been done away with I mean to see that his destroyers are punished."

"Quite right. That's my job too. But I'm gonna be real frank with you, miss. This here I X L outfit has had an unsavory reputation for twenty years. While I've never been able to git the proof I know in my own mind that it's always been a haunt for outlaws."

"I—I'm beginning to fear that is true," the girl faltered.

"Your brother was an Eastern chap, I take it?"

"Yes."

"Now mind you, I'm not inferrin' that this is what happened to him, but there have been lots of cases where rich young tenderfeet came out here, fell in with outlaws who got their money—an' were never heard from again."

Leda covered her face with her hands and gave an audible sob. The sheriff got up and gave her a fatherly pat on the shoulder.

"There, there, don't you give up hope thataway. If there's any help I can give you it's yours. But what I'm drivin' at is that this ain't no safe place for a girl. None whatever. Have you got any friends that you could stay with?"

She said nothing, because of her emotion, though she gripped the sheriff's big, rough hand gratefully.

"If yuh ain't," he said gently, "I've got a wife an' two daughters about yore age up in Newdale, an' we'd be plumb tickled tuh have you come live with us till yuh git straightened out."

Suddenly Leda found herself in complete command of her faculties and emotions. She wiped the tears out of her eyes and faced the sheriff with a smile.

"That's awfully kind of you, sheriff, and I appreciate it more than I can tell. But if we had to have a place to stay Mrs. Gemmell in Highriver has kindly offered us a home."

"You couldn't find a better place, nor a better friend," Wendall declared. "In fact, it was Nance Gemmell who asked me tuh look yuh up."

"But I'm convinced that something has happened to Charley, and so far as I can see the only possible chance I'll ever have to find out the truth is to stay right here. I'm not afraid."

"You're a mighty courageous girl," the sheriff said. "If you won't leave, though, I'll try to keep an eye on things. If I can ever help you any you let me know."

"I—I—hope that I'll be able to help a little too," she said hesitantly. "You see I—we—have already had a little experience with outlaws."

"When was that?" the sheriff asked quickly.

She told him about the hold-up in Penoloa canyon, and the subsequent return of their money.

"Now that's funny," Wendall said. "You say that the feller who stuck up the hold-ups themselves an' got back the money was ridin' with the same men the next day? What did them fellers look like?"

Leda gave him a detailed description of Kelvin, Biggers, and Fossum. A peculiar smile played over the sheriff's face.

"I wish I'd known that before," he said. "As a matter of fact, I had my hands on all three of them cusses after that. Had I known they went around terrorizin' wimmin an' kids I wouldn't uh let 'em slip away."

"But—but—one of them couldn't have been such a desperate character," she protested. "He returned our money." For some quite mysterious reason a deep blush overspread her face. The sheriff didn't fail to notice it.

"That speaks pretty well of the young feller," he said dubiously, "but it puts a lot o' leaks in another yarn. Me an' my posse had a gun battle with them an' another bunch, an' though some of my men was dead shore they saw this Kelvin shootin' at us when we got 'em rounded up we found him trussed up like a Christmas turkey, an' the yarn they told me was that he was a cattle buyer they'd been tryin' tuh swindle, an' they tied him up tuh keep him out o' danger. But if he held them up after they'd robbed you he musta knowed all the time that they was outlaws."

"I suppose he's an outlaw," the girl sighed, "but it's a shame. He really doesn't act like one."

"Yuh can't never tell, miss," the sheriff said soberly. "You'd be surprised at the upbringin' some of these Wild Ones have had. Most of 'em are just young loafers who've gone bad, but a number of 'em have been tuh college, an' more than one are from dang fine families. What's give 'em the wrong steer nobody knows, but in general they're the worst of the lot, because they have more sense."

The sheriff soon took his departure, but his last speech had brought apprehension to the girl's heart. Why she continued to think so much about Chet Kelvin she didn't know. That he was an outlaw with some good in him she couldn't doubt, but, she thought, he must be an outlaw none the less and, according to the sheriff, one of the more dangerous kind.

And the other suspicion that she had been trying to thrust from her as if it were an insidious poison had become more confirmed by the sheriff's visit. Unless Charley had been done away with by these outlaws, then it was almost certain that he had been one of them himself. The possibilities were equally tragic.

A couple of days later two other visitors appeared at the I X L. Both were striking-looking men, and Leda noted at once the deference with which they were treated by Adam Broome and his crew. One was a good-looking, tow-headed young fellow with baby-blue eyes and an easy, assured manner. The other was small, dark, and reticent. Yet both radiated force.

Leda tried to avoid all the men as much as possible, yet she knew it would defeat her own purpose if she withdrew to herself entirely. Whenever she was around the visitors the younger man stared at her so appraisingly out of those baby-blue eyes of his that she always felt her skin growing uncomfortably warm.

The men had gone when she arose the next morning, but they returned that night after dark. When she went to her room to retire that night she saw on the floor a scrap of dirty paper which had apparently been thrown or blown through her open window. She was about to throw it outside again when she noticed writing upon it. Somewhat wonderingly she spread it out and read:

"Dear Ledy. I bin trying awl day to see you alone but there ain't never bin no chance with out sum of these Fellers awatching of Us. don't dast lett on to nobody whut you Know but them Fellers ain't nobody Else but Kirk hoLLiDay and blacky pain. YoUrs tRUly neVaDa."

The information made Leda gasp, but not from fear. With every nerve tingling she resolved to get word to the sheriff of the presence here of the two outlaw leaders. She realized that doing so would be no easy job. Any move she made would be regarded with suspicion.

There was but one way that she could think of, and that was to drive boldly into Highriver and consult Nancy Gemmell. But to do that she would have to allay suspicion. She knew that

Bud wouldn't go to town with her anyway if he could help it. If she left him behind they would suspect nothing. It tore her heart to leave the boy among these outlaws for even an hour, but it seemed the only way to find out what had become of Charley.

EIGHTEEN

It was impossible not to feel sorry for Charley Harrison. Whatever he had been the man had pride. Perhaps the only thing in the world which tied him to the shreds of its self-respect was the love he had for his brother and sister. The desire to stand well in their eyes had caused him to lie to them about his high standing in the West, and now those lies had risen up to confound him.

A bitterer dose to swallow than the knowledge that Bud and Leda would now know that he was an outlaw and a liar would be hard to imagine. The grimace of mental agony on the man's face was too much for Chet to watch. He looked away.

"Thanks for telling me," Harrison said presently.

"I thought you'd better know," Chet said quietly. "There may be some way we can fix things up. If you'll be frank with me I'll do all I can."

"There's not much to tell," Harrison said with a hard laugh. "My folks were the finest people in the world, but I reckon I never was much good. I got into trouble back home and would have gone to prison there if my father hadn't come to my rescue.

"Anyway, I promised to come out West and make good." The man paused and gave a hollow laugh. "Make good! Yes; I made good all right—in a great big way."

"Why?" Chet asked sympathetically.

"I intended to do big things, all right," Harrison went on. "But it's not so easy when you haven't any capital but your bare hands. I drifted around a while, and ended up at the I X L ranch as a hay hand. Adam Broome paid me a dollar and a quarter a day and board. Back home I'd read of the doings of the famous Wild Ones. Here I knew I was on their stamping ground. I heard a lot about them. Some of 'em drifted in, and I talked with them. They told me about the easy money they made. It made my dollar and a quarter a day for ten hours of hard work look pretty small.

"That's about all. I helped with several jobs, got enough cash to be able to go home and put up a front, and being anxious to make the folks think I was doing all right I put up a bluff that I was the owner of the I X L. Oh, I know I was weak and foolish to do it, but it didn't seem that way then."

The man paused as though awaiting a comment, but as Chet had nothing to say he went on.

"I never got much out of it. I worked under Bobo Waite, and he got the lion's share of what we got. But even he had to divide up everything with a man named Bill Codd who runs a joint over at Highriver. Nobody can prove anything, but Codd is the real king of the outlaws in this section. And he has to divvy with Kirk Holliday.

"When we pulled that Soldier Summit job it made a big stir and we were hard pressed. We were trying to get back to Highriver, but Waite said we couldn't make it. He said for us all to split up, and told us where to go and where to meet later. Well, I found out later that he deliberately sent me to lead the posse away from the rest of them. I was caught, and they got away."

"And so yuh volunteered tuh lead the sheriff to 'em if yuh was paroled out of the penitentiary."

"That's about it, but I'm not quite as rotten as you think. I had sense enough finally to see where it had got me, and as soon as my contract with the state was finished I meant to go somewhere else and start over with a clean sheet."

The man's manner was so earnest, so devoid of pose and pretense that Chet believed him.

"But now it looks like the game was up with me anyway," Harrison went on. "I can't face my kid brother and sister. I simply can't. And now that they'll soon know what I am, I don't know that I mind having the Wild Ones know I'm working with the law."

"Now look here," Chet said sternly, "the trouble with you is you've never showed any backbone. And right now, when you need it more than ever, you're still short. Those kids are in a mess, but if I judged them right they'll stand by you if you tell them the same story you told me."

"I couldn't do it."

"Then what are you going to do—take a sneak and leave them to fight their way alone without a dollar or a friend?"

Harrison's shoulders straightened.

"No, by God, I won't," he declared. "I'll do something."

"Maybe I can help," Chet offered.

The other regarded him with a peculiar look. "Maybe you can—more than you think," he said enigmatically. It was a long time afterward before Chet sensed his real meaning.

"What do you want me to do?"

"I wonder if you'd mind finding out where Bud and Leda are and kind of keep an eye out for them? They'll be safe in Highriver, I think. Bill Codd knows that his place there means too much to him to risk pulling off any rough stuff. And if you get a chance you might mention to Leda that you've had a tip or something that I won't be coming back to this country soon."

"I'll do that," Chet promised, though a bit reluctantly. It seemed to him that Harrison's manner had altered considerably during the last five minutes. Why, he couldn't understand.

"Then if you'll do that, I'll leave you here," Harrison said. "What you've told me puts a different angle on my plans and the sheriff's. I must get in touch with him immediately."

"You know where to reach him?"

"That's the one thing that'll be easy," Harrison said. "If I was you I'd be mighty careful not to talk to strangers around here. Kirk Holliday will be after your scalp, but as I say, they won't dare try anything openly at Highriver or even at the I X L. But if they caught you between the two places it might be different."

"I'm bein' careful," Chet said grimly. "I'll be at Highriver, but if the sheriff needs any more men to go after Holliday's gang you tell him where to find me."

"I will."

They had reached the place where the trail forked, and here they separated. Harrison pointed out the trail Chet was to follow, and assured him that he could easily reach a camping place not far from the I X L ranch that night, and make it in to Highriver early the next morning.

Chet wasn't altogether satisfied with his interview with Charley Harrison. The last change in the man had been somewhat inexplicable. But his heart went out to Leda and Bud. Unless they believed that their brother was an outlaw—and he knew it would require a lot of proof to make them believe that, they might make themselves troublesome to the outlaws of Highriver. In either case they would be in danger, and Chet had seen enough of the Wild Ones to know that for all their claims to be followers of the tradition of Robin Hood and Dick Turpin there were cold-blooded killers among them, and even the leaders would stop at little if their schemes were thwarted.

That afternoon he had his first glance at the I X L ranch, and he realized that it was an ideal cow country. If young Charley Harrison had happened to accomplish what he claimed to his folks, how different it would have been for Bud and Leda now, he thought.

He made his camp that night a short distance from the creek which he knew must run through the I X L ranch. The timber was heavy, and he made a fire without fear, though he took his blankets a considerable distance away when he went to bed. The next morning he had breakfast early, and by sunrise he was on the edge of the naked red hills which lay between the I X L and Highriver.

Harrison had told him that he would have to cross an open flat within sight of the I X L buildings unless he made a detour of many miles, but it was far enough away that he wasn't likely to be identified even with glasses, and if he were he would be in the bad lands before he could possibly be overtaken.

He didn't hesitate, but started across the flat at a jog trot. Soon he could see the buildings quite plainly, but he saw no sign of anything to menace him.

The road was within reach but the danger of meeting some of the Wild Ones was too great for him to follow it if it could be avoided.

He was soon to find, however, that the deep washes and sheer banks between the rain-washed hills were almost an impassable barrier to one with no knowledge of the country. The road lay to his left, and though the country on the other side was higher and more rugged he believed that he could get above the heads of the washes on that side and get near enough to Highriver to make a quick dash in whenever he chose.

Finding a wash with sides too high and steep for his horse to climb he allowed the animal to pick its way downward over a hard-pan bottom that was as smooth and hard as an asphalt pavement. He didn't need to be told that the wagon road followed the main canyon where all these washouts converged. He was almost to the road, and was letting his mount pick its own gait, with the bridle reins looped carelessly over the saddle horn, when his ears caught the sound of wheels creaking and jolting over the bumpy road from the direction of the I X L.

He was instantly alert, and scooping up the reins with a swift dab, he reined his mount behind a shoulder of subsoil projecting into the wash. His position commanded a view of the road where it went up over a hummock after crossing the wash. He knew that he wouldn't be seen unless the driver chanced to look almost straight back.

Within five minutes the rig he had heard jostled down into the wash, ground across the deposit of gravel which marked the crossing, and lurched up the other side into view. Chet's withheld breath popped out with an explosive gasp.

He had seen that buckboard before, and its sole occupant at present was Leda Harrison!

He was suddenly mastered by an irresistible impulse to talk with her. Without giving himself time for second thought, he spurred down into the road and quickly overhauled the buckboard. He was less than three rods behind when the girl heard him coming, and looked back. His appearance had unexpectedly startling results.

Looking back over her shoulder the girl recognized Chet, and surprise so overcame her that she uttered an exclamation, and allowed her tight grip on the lines to relax. The word and the quick release of the bits were interpreted by the ponies as a desire for more speed. Being cayuse bred, their recuperative faculties were amazing, and a few days' rest had made them rollicky. They leaped ahead, jerking the leather through the girl's fingers. The buckboard struck a band and careened. The ponies looked back and saw a horseman behind them, and they pretended to get scared.

In less than a rod they were stretched out and running like greyhounds.

NINETEEN

THE STAMPEDE of Snip and Coley was as unexpected to Chet as it was to Leda, but he had dropped the roan pacer's leading rope and sunk the rowels into Mike's hide at the first jump. He rightly ascribed the runaway to a spirit of pure cayuse deviltry, and not to genuine fright; but like little boys the ponies had a faculty for giving themselves a terrible scare.

Ordinarily there would have been little or no danger, for they would soon tire of running and drop back into a trot. But the road, plunging in and out of a succession of washes, was treacherous and there was imminent danger of the rig being upset. The girl might be seriously injured if she were thrown out, or if she jumped.

"Don't jump, Leda—just try to hold 'em in the road," he yelled.

She didn't answer, but he saw that she had no intention of jumping. She had gathered up the lines and was pulling back with all her strength. But the runaways had the bits in their teeth and she had as well have tried to hold the wind.

At the first leap her hat had blown off, and as it struck the ground in front of Chet's horse it caused that animal to kink himself into a knot which would have unseated any ordinary rider. A little later Leda's flaxen tresses were flying loosely in the breeze, and the rider couldn't help admiring the picture she made, despite the fear he felt for her safety.

Once the front of the buckboard ran far up the bank, and it seemed that it would surely tip over. It righted itself, however, and the girl clung to her seat, though she was almost thrown over the dashboard.

Fast as the Mike horse was he gained slowly on the swift-flying cayuses. It was a hot race for a quarter of a mile before he was able to draw abreast and grab Coley's outside check. But once he got the horse's head twisted sideways he was quickly able to bring the team to a plunging stop. He looked back as he was stopping them and saw that the girl's face was red. When he got them completely stopped it was white.

"Onery little cusses," he said. "Hope they didn't scare you. Rotten careless of me comin' up on yuh the way I did."

"I—I—didn't have time to get scared till now," she smiled. "I'm afraid I'm not much of a driver."

"You done fine to hold 'em in the road," he assured her. "I think they'll be all right now, but tuh make sure I'll fix 'em so they can be held." He dismounted and proceeded to run the check straps through the bit rings and snapped them into the halters; thus giving the driver a double purchase on them.

"That'll hold 'em for a while," he grinned. "Now I'll ride back an' git yore hat."

He swung lithely into the saddle and turned his horse, but the girl cried:

"Wait!"

He paused by the front wheel of the rig with an inquiring look upon his face.

"Were you going to Highriver?" she asked, flushing.

"That was my destination," he admitted, "providing something don't happen tuh stop me on the way."

"You seem to have the habit of showing up just when I'm needing help badly." She smiled a little. "I owe you a debt of gratitude. I—I—must tell you that I'm going to Highriver to get into communication with the sheriff."

For a moment Chet was puzzled. Then it dawned upon him that she was giving him a warning. She still believed that he was a member of the Wild Ones. And he realized, too, that he couldn't make her think otherwise in view of his association with Fossum and Biggers.

"That's nice of you," he said. "I was kinda lookin' for the sheriff myself."

The girl's eyes widened. "Maybe you don't understand," she offered. "I know that the sheriff let you go the other day because you and your friends made him believe you were a victim of the outlaws. But I had a talk with him later, and when I told him what I knew, he—he decided that he'd been fooled."

"I see."

"But I told him how you had made those others give our money back," she said quickly, and a bit defensively.

"Have you heard any news of yore brother?"

"No-o. That is, I don't know where he is now. But I do know that he is the owner of the I X L ranch," she said triumphantly.

"Yuh—what?" he blurted.

"I know he's the owner of the I X L," she repeated. "The former owner, Adam Broome, admitted that himself. My brother is somewhere in the East raising money to pay for it. Bud and I are waiting there till he comes back."

"At the I X L?"

"Yes. And if he doesn't come back, then there can be but one reason. These—these outlaws may have killed him."

Chet was utterly astounded. That the outlaws had lied to this girl and got her to stay at the I X L ranch to his mind spelled but one thing: They had some ulterior motive which augured no good for her and Bud. But she believed him an outlaw, and would pay no attention to any warning he might give. Nor could he come out bluntly and tell her the truth—that her brother was even then but a few miles away.

"Miss Harrison, I have just been among some of these outlaws, and I heard them mention yore brother," he said. "I know positively that they haven't done away with him."

"Oh, oh, thank you for telling me that," she breathed.

"You were kind enough to give me a warning just now," he went on. "I appreciate the spirit of that more than you know. I want to make some return, so I'm goin' tuh give you one."

"I'm not afraid of these Wild Ones," she said, lifting her rounded chin a bit stubbornly.

"Not for yoreself, of course," he said. "But have you considered what the Wild Ones might do to yore brother if they happened to get you or Bud, or both of you, in their power?"

He hated to frighten her, but he believed honestly that in no other way could he persuade her to leave the I X L. That she was in danger there he was firmly convinced. He could tell by her whitening cheeks that he had impressed her. And because she believed that he was one of the gang she wouldn't doubt that he knew what he was talking about.

"You—you—mean that they might abduct one of us and make Charley pay a big ransom for our release?" she faltered.

"They could take him for every dollar he's got," Chet said. Emboldened by the success of his deception, he added brazenly: "No doubt the danger of that very thing is the reason he never sent for you and Bud."

"Oh, now I begin to understand." The blood seemed to have all ebbed from the girl's face. Chet suddenly feared that he had scared her more than he had intended.

"Of course—" he began diffidently.

"I'm beginning to understand now," she murmured, and there was a mute look of appeal in her glorious eyes as she looked at him. "I've got to go back to the ranch at once. It's funny I never once thought that the presence of that outlaw leader, Kirk Holliday, had anything to do with me."

"What do you mean?" he asked.

"I don't know whether you know it or not, but Kirk Holliday himself has been hanging around the I X L for several days with another man who Nevada says is his chief aide. I—I—felt that it was my duty to find the sheriff and tell him about their being there. That's where I was going. But Bud is there alone. This—this may be their opportunity to seize him. I must go back. Where can I turn around?"

"Just a minute," Chet pleaded. "I think you'd ought to go back and get Bud all right, and go somewhere where you'll be safe. But I'm quite sure there's no danger today. They'll want you both, and they wouldn't have let you come into town had they intended tuh do anything now. But I do think you ought to go back an' git Bud on some pretext, an' git away from there."

"I will. I can see the necessity for it now," she said. "We'll move in with Mrs. Gemmell in Highriver and wait for Charley. I know we'll be safe there."

Chet had achieved what he had set out to do. For the present all he could hope for was to get Leda and Bud away from the I X L, and he couldn't regret frightening the girl a bit if it achieved that result.

"Better just tell 'em the team run away—they show that—an' say you were afraid to drive them all the way alone. That'll give you an excuse to bring Bud back with you," he advised.

"Thank you, I will," she said. "And you?"

"I think I'll still try to see the sheriff," he smiled.

"I—I—wish you would," she said. "He's a just man, and if you would only—only change your ways I don't believe you—you'd regret it."

Chet helped her turn the buckboard around, collected her hat, and restored it to her. Then he watched her drive out of sight.

With a peculiar sigh, for which he could assign no particular reason, he rode back up the wash and got the roan pacer.

What the outlaws' game could be in deluding the girl about her brother's alleged ownership of the I X L he couldn't imagine, but suddenly he determined to find out. His interview with the sheriff could wait. With a cluck of the tongue to his horses he turned and rode boldly along the road toward Highriver.

He had heard enough from the outlaws themselves to know that the most powerful man, in this county at least, next to Kirk Holliday himself was a man named Bill Codd. This Codd, he understood, wasn't an active outlaw, but rather a fence for the outlaws.

105

As yet Codd had never seen him; perhaps had no idea what he looked like. Undoubtedly Holliday and Payne had told the man that Chet was a prisoner in the hide-out at Stag-tail butte, so Codd shouldn't suspect his true identity. There were so many members of the Wild Ones in the three or four states in which the gang operated that it would be impossible for the man Codd to have seen them all unless he rode with the outlaws himself. If he could make the man believe that he was a Wild One, he might be able to get the information he desired.

The town of Highriver was less than a mile away when he came in sight of it. It was a drab enough looking place despite its brave show of being an oasis in that unbroken expanse of vermilion-colored hills.

Close at hand was a shady clump of junipers. It occurred to Chet that it might be advisable for him to postpone his entrance into the town until after dark. He could also watch the road and see whether Bud and Leda arrived. If they didn't show up it would be proof that they had been forcibly prevented. It was tiresome waiting, but he knew that it was perhaps as cool in the junipers as anywhere else.

It was past the middle of the afternoon when the grinding of wheels caused him to look back up the road. It was Leda and Bud Harrison in the buckboard, and Chet could see by the discontented look upon Bud's face that the boy resented being dragged back to town.

When it became dark enough to prevent his horses being identified easily by any chance member of the Wild Ones who might have happened to see them, he rode into the town.

It was easy enough to locate Bill Codd's establishment. He encountered a man in the street and was directed around to the rear of the livery stable. A solitary attendant responded to his hail.

"Put my horses up an' then tell yore boss that I'd like to have a talk with him in a back room," Chet ordered. "I have reasons for not goin' in the front way."

"I wonder if the name o' that reason is Wendall?" the hostler asked with a laugh.

"What about him? Is he here?" Chet demanded with every evidence of alarm.

"He shore is," the man replied.

Chet mouthed a disgusted oath. "Damned lucky I didn't go in the front, I guess," he said.

As the man swung his lantern about it fell upon the two horses. Without appearing to watch Chet saw the man look the animals over closely.

"Ever been here before?" the man asked, as he led the horses into the stable.

106

"Never. I'm a stranger in the country. I was told tuh see Bill Codd."

"Well, foller me," the man bade, and led the way to the rear of the cluster of ramshackle buildings which composed the domicile of Bill Codd.

They passed around one of these buildings and went into a two-foot alleyway between it and another. They entered the second building, which was dark, tramped across a bare floor, and entered another room. Here Chet's guide lit a lamp, revealing that they were in a sort of office. A battered rolltop desk stood in one corner, and some shelves were cluttered with a miscellany of papers and books, mostly dusty old account books. There was a table in the middle of the room, and a few chairs.

"Wait here," the man said, and disappeared through another door. Chet glanced around coolly, and sat down on one corner of the desk. A few minutes later the door opened, and an incredibly fat man waddled into the room. The man's skin was a yellowish color from too much indoor living, and he had shaved so carelessly that his face resembled a hog recently scalded and scraped. Indeed, save for the small, glittering eyes which peered out from behind rolls of fat, the whole face seemed peculiarly that of a dead animal.

The stableman was with the man, but he hurried across the room and halted at the other door.

"You wanted to see me?" the fat man challenged.

Chet slid off the table corner and stood erect. In height he dominated the other man by ten inches.

"You're Bill Codd?"

"That's my name," the fat man said coldly, and then added, as though he might be addressing the hostler, "Where's George?"

With a perfectly straight face Chet answered: "In the Bosom of Abraham."

TWENTY

THE EXPRESSION on Bill Codd's face altered instantly when Chet unhesitatingly gave the password which had served him on a previous occasion. The fat man stuck out an enormous, flabby paw.

"Where yuh from an' what's yore monicker?" he wanted to know.

"I'm from up Powder river way," Chet replied. "I'm known as Cherokee Fisher." He had given the name of a notorious Southwest outlaw who he had reason to know was doing time in the Kansas penitentiary.

"Seems like I've heard the name before, but I don't recall any o' the boys I know usin' it," the man said as he dropped into his big office chair with a grunt and signaled Chet to sit down.

"Maybe not," Chet said coolly. "I'm not exactly one of these Wild Ones."

"But—"

"There's nothin' tuh git excited about," Chet said calmly. "I'm huntin' for Kirk Holliday tuh join up with him. I've been doin' time in the Kansas pen, but I broke out six months ago, an' been on the dodge ever since. I worked my way up into Wyoming, hopin' tuh git in touch with the Wild Ones, an outfit I've heard a lot about. I met several fellers I knew who belonged to it. They told me Holliday was down this way at present an' give me the password, that's all."

"It may be all, but it may not be enough," Codd said. "There's been some damned spies around here lately."

"I know that," Chet said. "As a matter of fact I was asked tuh warn you an' Holliday about a feller who goes by the name of Chet Kelvin, an' poses as a cattle buyer."

"Yeah? What about him?" Codd asked eagerly.

"He's a fake, that's all."

"I thought so," Codd hissed. "I've done heard about that feller already. I don't think we need worry about him no more, but what we would like tuh know is who-all is workin' with him. Ever hear of a man called Dude Johnson?"

"Johnson? I run across a feller named 'Butch' Johnson, but he never would be called Dude. What about him?"

"He's the hombre we suspect has passed out all the information tuh this detective Kelvin, and to Jay Wendall. We've got reason tuh think he's back in the country."

"I'm afraid I can't help yuh out any there," Chet said. "But I would like tuh git in touch with Holliday."

"Too bad yuh didn't git here a day sooner. Holliday an' Blackie Payne were right here last night. But they've gone back tuh their headquarters now, an' it's almost a two-day ride."

"Well, I ain't crowded for time," Chet laughed. "What I want mostly is a place tuh lay by an' rest for a day or two—where I can keep outa the way o' sheriffs. Yore hostler tells me yuh've got one underfoot here now."

The saloonman's voice became tinged with venom. "Yes, damn him. He knows I can't git up an' travel, so he planks down here an' makes himself at home whenever he pleases."

"I wonder how much it'd be worth tuh have somethin' happen tuh that said sheriff?" Chet asked dreamily.

Codd's head lifted with a jerk. "It'd be worth a thousand dollars tuh me—if it was done right," he said.

"How d'ye mean right?"

"Are you offerin' tuh git him—if the price is right?"

"Such things has been done," Chet said laconically. "He kin be reached—an' I kin use some money."

"It can't be done here," the saloonkeeper said in a whisper. "I couldn't afford tuh have anything like that happen. But I would like tuh have the old devil out of the way. My case is different from Holliday's, Fisher. He ain't tied tuh no one place. All my interests are here, an' lately I've been gittin' worried. Holliday don't want any officers killed off because it only puts others on his trail."

"But you have personal an' private reasons for wantin' tuh git rid of this particular sheriff," Chet murmured.

"Right. I've stood Wendall off for years, but for the first time I can't figger out his game."

"How's that?" Chet asked casually, though inwardly he was excited. He seemed to have won this fat scoundrel's confidence. He wondered what further revelations would be forthcoming.

"First, are you willing to undertake the job?" Codd demanded bluntly.

"Not for a thousand dollars," Chet said drily. "Make it worth my while an' I'll go gunnin' for yore sheriff."

Codd's latent suspicion seemed to return. "How do I know you're not a damned detective yoreself?" he hissed.

"Yuh don't," Chet said. "All you've got is my word. But send for Blackie Payne or anybody else that knows anything about Cherokee Fisher an' I'll damn' soon convince yuh." In his experience on the cattle trails Chet had more than once came into contact with the outlaw he was impersonating. And from Jack Fossum he had learned many intimate details about the Wild Ones—details he could have secured from no other source. He proceeded to mention men and events with such casual certitude that he could see conviction settling over the fat man's face. Besides that, Codd wanted to believe.

"I reckon yo're all right," Codd said finally. "Yore story rings true. Kill me a sheriff, an' yuh kin name yore own price—if it's anything in reason. Only yuh mustn't do it here."

"Five hundred dollars cash now, and a thousand when the job is finished," Chet said.

Codd didn't part with five hundred dollars easily, but at last he lumbered out and returned with the bills.

"Just why are yuh so anxious tuh git this particular sheriff?" Chet asked, as he crammed the bills into his pocket.

"For one reason he refuses tuh let me alone," the man said discontentedly. "But while he fought fair I didn't mind so much.

Now he's bringin' wimmin an' kids into the row, an' I don't know what it means."

"Just how do yuh mean?" Chet asked.

"Just this: There's a big ranch out here called the I X L which belongs to a friend o' mine named Adam Broome. Fact is I've got quite a claim on the property. Well, right recently a girl an' her kid brother showed up here claimin' the I X L belongs tuh a brother o' theirs. The fust thing they done is hunt up ole lady Gemmell, an old woman who lives across the street here an' who hates me an' Broome like the devil does holy water."

"Yuh mean tuh say they're claimin' this ranch with no evidence of title?" Chet asked with pretended amazement.

"That's the hell of it," the fat man admitted. "I—we—that is, Adam Broome owns it. Got good title an' everything. But all this sudden activity, bringin' in detectives, gittin' Dude Johnson let outa the pen an' all that, indicates that old Wendall is hell-bent tuh git somethin' on us. If he does an' this here gal makes a claim that this imaginary brother o' hers owned the ranch an' lays a claim that the Wild Ones killed him off they might make it stick in spite of Adam's title."

"Do you mean tuh say that this Adam Broome mebbe did pretend tuh sell the I X L tuh the girl's brother, and then—"

"Hell, no," Codd interrupted impatiently. "The whole thing is a plot that's been cooked up between old lady Gemmell an' Jay Wendall. That's why I wanta git rid o' the sheriff. When that's accomplished I reckon I kin deal with Nance Gemmell."

"Say, I believe I'd orta raise my price," Chet drawled.

Codd became instantly a changed man. His bulky body tensed angrily; his mean little eyes from behind their arbors of overhanging fat glistened with suspicion.

"Don't try holdin' me up, feller," he said angrily. "I may be afraid o' sheriffs, but I kin deal with any damned outlaw that ever come down the pike."

"Keep yore shirt on," Chet laughed. "I wanta join up with Kirk Holliday. This here job of fixin' a sheriff's clock is just an incident tuh me. Besides, it's the kind o' work I like tuh do."

"All right then," Codd said, somewhat mollified. "Now I'll tell yuh what yuh do. Wendall ain't in the saloon now, but he'll soon be back I reckon. When he comes I'll show him to yuh. Then tomorrer, when he leaves, you kin foller him. But don't be in no hurry about takin' a shot at him. If yuh kin, try an' see who he meets."

"Don't worry about me," Chet said easily.

Perhaps twenty minutes later a little bell jingled right under the saloonkeeper's desk. Chet gave a little involuntary start, and grinned sheepishly.

"I reckon that's him now," Codd said and heaved his vast bulk upright. With a jerk of his thumb toward Chet, the man waddled over to the wall, removed a coat hanging innocently upon a nail, and using the nail as a knob thrust aside a small sliding panel. The panel commanded a view of the saloon, and it was so placed that it couldn't be noticed from the other side. Codd's office was considerably above the level of the saloon floor.

In a whisper Codd informed Chet which was the sheriff. The latter pretended to have difficulty fixing his gaze upon the right man, but presently got it straight. Codd closed the panel and lumbered over to the door.

"I'll show you yore room now, an' on the way I'll show yuh the sheriff's. If yuh'd ruther I'll send yuh up some supper."

"That'll be fine," Chet said. They went into a small hall, ascended a short flight of stairs and walked back along a corridor.

"Here's yore room," Codd said, "an' the one right across the hall is Wendall's."

Chet had been far luckier in obtaining information than he had even dared to hope when he entered the town, but at the same time he realized that he had put himself in a lot more danger, and he already was in plenty.

If anyone recognized him or his horses, or if he was caught speaking with either the sheriff or the Harrisons, Codd would know how he had been tricked. In that event he knew that the obese saloonkeeper would be as deadly and treacherous as an Apache. But he couldn't withdraw from the position he had assumed even if he wanted to. The only thing to do was lay low and try to get in touch with the sheriff.

Half an hour later a waiter came up with a tray containing an ample meal. Chet dismissed the man, and asked him not to come for the empty dishes until morning. He left his door slightly opened, and listened for the sheriff as he ate.

He had just finished when he heard a heavy tread coming down the corridor. It was Sheriff Wendall, but Chet dared not take the chance then of attracting his attention. He knew that Wendall might be followed. It also occurred to him that Codd might have told him which was Wendall's room just to see what he would do. With the place full of trick doors and sliding panels it was too dangerous to take chances.

Finally he wrote a brief note. "Meet me in the coulee above the nearest clump of junipers northeast of town the first thing in the morning. This is important." After a moment of deliberation he signed his name to it.

He got up and dressed at four o'clock the next morning. It was just beginning to get light. Slipping out of his room on

111

tiptoe he listened cautiously at the sheriff's door; then knelt as though trying to peer through the keyhole. While in this position he contrived to slip the note under the door. Then he got to his feet and moved silently down the still dark corridor.

At the head of the stairs he confronted Bill Codd. Where the man had materialized from he had no idea, but he was certain he had been seen at the sheriff's door. But whether Codd had observed him thrusting the note under the door he didn't know. If he had—then he could expect things to break dangerously before he could get away from the place.

"Where are you goin'?" Codd asked. His tone wasn't reassuring.

"Downstairs, an' I'll talk tuh you," Chet whispered impatiently.

Without a word the fat man stood aside for him to go down first. At the landing Chet stood and waited until Codd eased his huge body down the stairway.

"I don't want anybody around here to see me, so I'm ridin' out a little ways to where I can see which way the sheriff leaves an' be able tuh follow him," he explained.

"Good idee, I reckon," Codd agreed, and Chet knew then that he hadn't seen the note. But he knew that if he had tried to talk with the sheriff that night he would have been spied upon. It had been rather a close call.

He again became secretly alarmed when Codd insisted upon lumbering out to the stable with him. If a description of his horses had been given the man, then the only thing left to do would be to bash him over the head and make his getaway before he came to.

The hostler was sound asleep, as his loud snores testified, and at Chet's insistence he wasn't awakened.

"I can get my own horses as well as he can," he declared.

"Where'd yuh git the little roan?" Codd asked interestedly as Chet led the animals out.

"I traded for him," Chet said guardedly. "I don't know whether the man who owned him liked the trade or not."

Codd grinned his appreciation. "Yuh know I'd like a little pony like that," he said wistfully. "One I could climb onto, an' was easy-gaited. I don't git enough exercise. I'm gittin' too fat."

"Then this is just the horse you want," Chet said. "He's a pacer. When I git back I'll talk trade with you."

He swung upon Mike and rode away. Bill Codd's eyes were fixed upon the roan pacer. He had scarcely noticed the gray.

Chet headed at once for the clump of junipers which he had passed the previous afternoon, but he kept on going until he was in the coulee above, where he had requested the sheriff to meet him. Leaving his horses, he returned to a point from whence he could watch the town.

It was fully three hours before he saw Sheriff Wendall ride away, and the officer headed across the bench on the main road toward Boxtown. Chet was in for an anxious half hour or so. But at the end of that time he heard the scuffling of stones, and presently the sheriff came in sight down another draw. The officer had made a sweeping semicircle.

"Well, my young outlaw, what do you wanta see me about?" were the sheriff's first words.

"I thought yuh might be interested in knowin' that Bill Codd paid me five hundred dollars last night to put the bee on you," Chet answered laconically.

TWENTY-ONE

SHERIFF WENDALL's busy white eyebrows lifted with surprise at Chet's calm announcement, but he betrayed no fear.

"You wouldn't lie tuh me, would yuh, younker?" he queried.

"Well, not this time," Chet responded. "But it has been done."

"So I noticed," the sheriff said grimly. "You an' Jack Fossum pulled the wool over my eyes in fine shape that day. But we'll let that pass. Now what's this about Bill Codd?"

Chet produced the packet of bills he had received from Codd. "My advance for bumping you off," he explained.

"If Bill Codd's gone tuh hirin' men tuh dry-gulch me he's worse scared than I thought," Wendall said. "But why ain't you tryin' tuh earn yore money?"

"I wish I could make you understand that I'm not, an' never have been a Wild One." Chet frowned. "I'm just what I claimed to be—Chet Kelvin, an Idaho cattle buyer."

"Go on," Wendall grinned. "I like tall stories."

"That's the hell of it," Chet. objected. "I'm tellin' you the truth, but you think I'm an outlaw, an' the damned outlaws think I'm a detective, all except Bill Codd, an' he thinks I'm a killer from Kansas anxious tuh practice my trade."

"Go ahead an' talk," Wendall grunted, "but I'm a hard hombre tuh fool—the second time."

Chet talked. He related what had happened to him from the time he had met Jack Fossum and Al Biggers in Curryville until he had left Codd's hotel that morning.

The sheriff listened with a skeptical smile.

"It's a good story," Wendall said, "but you'd better go back an' tell Bill Codd that I don't believe it."

"But I want tuh help you," Chet protested. "I want to help that girl. I've had experience with men like Holliday an' Payne before. If you'd look up my record you'd find out that I am telling you the truth. Why, there ain't an officer or a stockman anywhere along the trail from Texas to Montana who don't know me."

"Yeah? Well, I ain't lived in this county all my life an' I'm purty well known along that trail myself," Wendall said shortly. "An' I ain't never heard the name Kelvin before."

"Mebbe not, but yuh must've heard of Tornado Tex," Chet said impatiently.

"What?" the sheriff roared. "Are you meanin' tuh tell me yo're Tornado Tex?"

"That's the fool name they hung onto me," Chet admitted. "I've been tryin' tuh live it down. I don't claim tuh be a tornado, an' I wasn't raised in Texas."

"Well, my friend, I've heard plenty about Tornado Tex," Wendall said. "If you are him I reckon you can prove it. I never saw the man, but I was in Livingston about three years ago when the cattlemen's association was buyin' a gold watch for Tornado Tex in appreciation of him wipin' out a gang that had been murderin' their men along the trail an' stealin' a lot of cattle. I didn't see the man, but I did see the watch, an' I'd know it again if I seen it."

Without a word Chet pulled out his watch and handed it to the sheriff. The officer examined it minutely, and extended his hand.

"Shake," he said. "Now I can understand how you come tuh git away from Kirk Holliday's men."

"That was mostly luck," Chet laughed. "I've been in a tougher spot right along than I wanted to be, but now that I'm in it I'd like to see it through."

"You'll git yore chance," the sheriff said. "What I'm out tuh do is land Bill Codd an' his particular crowd of cutthroats, Bobo Waite an' the others, behind the bars. If I can do that I can make my county too hot tuh hold Kirk Holliday an' his Wild Ones even if I can't arrest 'em."

"But why not git the whole gang?" Chet demanded. "I know where their hide-out is. Raise a posse an' go after 'em."

"Can't be done." The sheriff shrugged. "In the first place, Stag-tail butte ain't in my county. In the second place, no jury in this country would convict Holliday of anything short of murder, an' he's careful not tuh let us git him for that. That's why Codd had tuh appeal tuh you tuh kill me. People are either afraid tuh convict him, or else they think he's a kind of romantic hero an' won't. But I have the goods on Bobo Waite, an' if I could git him I might also git Codd."

114

"What about Charley Harrison?"

"Well, now that he knows they're onto him I reckon we won't see him no more, an' I don't know that I blame him. I was tuh meet him tonight at Nance Gemmell's place. He may be there so I'll have tuh keep the appointment."

"At Mrs. Gemmell's?" Chet exclaimed. "If he comes there he'll find his sister and brother!"

"H-m, well, I'll try tuh be there an' prevent that if I can," the sheriff said. "It might be darned humiliatin' for him, an' painful tuh them."

"Listen, sheriff. Why can't you strain a point an' let Leda an' Bud believe that their brother had been a spy for you all along?" Chet pleaded.

" 'Fraid not," Wendall said. "If he had tuh git on the witness stand an' swear tuh a lot o' lies it might undo all I've hoped tuh accomplish. The question is now, what're we gonna do about corrallin' the Bobo Waite gang? After that we'll have tuh see if we can't git back that twenty-five thousand dollars you lost."

"I'm afraid that's gone," Chet said ruefully. "But I have got a little plan that might work tuh nab yore men."

"Let's have it."

"Suppose I ride back tuh Highriver tonight with yore badge, an' mebbe yore blood-soaked vest, an' claim that other thousand dollars. Unless Codd has wised up tuh me he'll tell me a lot of things—probably enough tuh put the screws on him when you show up big as life the next morning. No fat man wants tuh go tuh jail, an' you'd orta be able tuh make him bring the other men yuh want into yore trap."

"You'd be takin' an awful chance, Kelvin," the sheriff objected. "Suppose Codd has been notified about yuh gittin' away? Yuh won't be able tuh fool him the next time."

"But if he does know the truth an' thinks I'm lyin' to him, he won't dare do nothin' tuh me because then he'll figure yo're watchin' every move he makes."

"You may be right," the sheriff said admiringly. "Anyway, I'll put in the rest o' the day gatherin' up a posse I can depend on. An' me an' eight or ten men will be right close around when yuh go in there."

The sheriff rode away, and Chet went a little farther into the hills, but he had the sheriff's badge and the gray, striped vest which Wendall always wore. The badge was fastened so that it wouldn't easily come off, and Chet didn't disturb it. There could be no question but that it was the sheriff's property. During the day he shot a rabbit and let a goodly share of its blood soak into the vest.

It was again after dark when he entered Highriver. If it had been dangerous before, it was doubly so now. Yet he stabled his horses and knocked on the door of Bill Codd's private office as nonchalantly as though nothing of importance had happened.

It seemed to him that the fat man's manner was unduly nervous when he appeared.

"You back already? I wasn't expectin' yuh," the man said.

"It don't take me all year tuh do a job," Chet bragged.

"Yuh mean tuh say"—Codd's voice dropped to a hoarse whisper—"that yuh got him?"

"Are we strictly alone?" Chet asked.

Codd dropped heavily into his chair. "Absolutely alone," he said, his little beady eyes boring into Chet's unblinkingly. "What happened?"

"Plenty—from Wendall's point of view," Chet laughed. He produced the bloodstained vest and badge and laid them on the desk under the saloonkeeper's nose.

Codd examined the articles in minute detail. "Where?" he asked.

"About twenty miles up the river. I threw his body into the stream."

"Yuh did, eh?" The fat man gave an evil chuckle. He seemed inordinately pleased about something.

"I did," Chet said coldly. "Now what about that thousand dollars?"

"I reckon yuh've earned it," Codd said. "I'll git it for yuh."

"Just a minute," Chet remonstrated. "The job's done, an' I want my pay. But that's only half of it. I want a place where I can hide out for a few weeks before announcin' myself."

"That's all right. I know just the place. It's where Bobo Waite an' his men have been hangin' out for a long time. Perfectly safe. It's likely they're back there right now. I'll send George Tandy along tuh show yuh the road an' interduce yuh."

"You give me the directions an' I'll find my way without no guide," Chet asserted.

"Just as you say," Codd assented. He lumbered out, but quickly returned with the thousand dollars. He dropped down in his chair, panting from the exertion of walking, and then began to thumb out the bills.

Chet had unconsciously leaned ahead in his chair and his eyes were upon the fat man's pudgy fingers. Suddenly some sixth sense warned him of danger. He started to turn, but he was an instant too late. Something hard and heavy crashed down upon his head with terrific force. He was stunned, and flashes of fire shot before his eyes, but with a stupendous effort he managed to get his hands on the arms of his chair and lift himself up.

He had got six inches from the chair when the loaded hose

descended the second time. This time everything went black, and he slumped back into his chair, his head falling upon the desk.

Deliberately Bill Codd went through his victim's pockets and collected the five hundred dollars he had previously given him.

"Load him into the democrat wagon an' haul him out tuh the I X L," the saloonkeeper addressed the stocky wielder of the blackjack. "An' you, Tandy, hustle over an' tell Kirk Holliday if he wants his detective tuh come an' git him. If he don't want him, we'll know what tuh do with him. An' tell Adam Broome tuh send this hombre down tuh the Red Water hole as soon as he's able tuh ride a horse."

TWENTY-TWO

LEDA HARRISON'S reaction to the welcome she received from Mrs. Gemmell was one of pure joy. Until she came to the safe harbor of that broad but sheltering bosom she hadn't realized the strain she had been under at the I X L. To her own amazement she sobbed unrestrainably for a few minutes before she could speak a word.

"What's wrong, honey? Has anything happened out there to worry you?" Mrs. Gemmell demanded.

"No, everything has been quite all right." Leda smiled. "It's strange, of course, but I can't complain of my treatment. I—I—had a runaway coming in. I guess that's what upset my nerves."

The explanation didn't pass muster with Mrs. Gemmell. "Leppy," she called. "Come help Bud take care o' their team. You'll stay with me a while, o' course?" she questioned Leda.

"I think I will," Leda smiled gratefully. "I've been horribly lonesome."

Old Leppy stumbled out, blinking his eyes like an owl startled into flight in daylight, and took charge of Snip and Coley. Leda followed the landlady into the cool, restful house.

"Any news of yore brother?" Nancy queried.

"In a way. The reason we came here was because I got a warning from the same outlaw who once returned my money that they might be going to kidnap one or both of us to make Charley pay them ransom."

" 'Bout time yuh come here then," Nancy said. But she was more mystified than ever.

It was considerably after bedtime when Nancy heard a light tapping at her window. It took more than that to scare her, but she gripped the revolver under her pillow as she demanded in a low voice to know who it was.

117

"It's me, Nancy—Jay Wendall. I want a room, but I don't wanta come in yore front door."

"All right, hoist yoreself through the winder, but don't make any more noise than yuh can help. I'd hate tuh lose my reputation after all these years."

The sheriff scrambled into the room with a considerable amount of puffing. "Not as young as I used tuh be," he apologized.

"Maybe that's lucky for me," Nancy said drily. "What's up?"

"I want yore front room. You see I'm half expectin' a caller, an' I want the front door open so he won't have tuh make any noise gittin' in."

"Help yourself," Nancy said. "That boy and girl are here tonight. Some outlaw who seems to have a case on Leda warned her that she might be kidnapped. There's a lot of fishy things goin' on around here. Do you know anything about it?"

"I know plenty," the sheriff said in a low voice. "The outlaw who warned her ain't an outlaw at all. He's an outlaw fighter. But the precious brother she's so worried about has been one, though he's been workin' with me for some time."

"I was almost certain that this Charley Harrison had been an outlaw."

"It so happens," the sheriff said, "that he's the very man I've got an appointment with here tonight."

"Good Lord!" Nancy exclaimed. "We mustn't let 'em meet."

"I'll be careful," the sheriff said.

It was almost midnight when the light-sleeping sheriff heard the front door open cautiously. He got up from the cot on which he had been lying fully dressed and gripped his gun.

"Who's there?" he challenged softly.

"That you, sheriff?" a voice asked.

"Yes; I'll strike a light." Wendall had seen to it that the blinds were down. As he lighted the lamp his gaze fell upon the nervous figure of Charley Harrison.

"Well, Dude, I really didn't expect yuh."

"No? Why?"

"I just had an idea you'd quit the country. Don't know's I'd have blamed yuh either. Yuh see I've had a talk with Chet Kelvin."

"Uh-huh. I guessed that. Well, I'm here. I suppose you know that my usefulness to you is ended. The Wild Ones are onto me."

"I'm afraid they are. Why did you come back?"

"Because my kid sister and brother are here, Wendall. I want to ask you to look out for 'em until I can get out of the country. Then I'll write back and tell 'em to come home."

"An' will you be there to meet 'em?"

"That's up to you," Harrison said. "If you tell 'em the truth I won't be."

"You'll be breakin' yore parole."

"I can't help it," the man said stubbornly.

"Maybe yo're right at that," Wendall said. "If it was just you, I wouldn't hear of it. Need any money?"

"No. And I'll pay you back for every cent you spend on them."

"Look here, Dude, you ain't been crossin' me, have you?" the sheriff demanded severely.

"Why should I?" Harrison shrugged.

"No reason, I guess. But before you go I thought mebbe yuh'd like tuh know that yore kinfolks are here tonight."

"God, I wish I could see them," the man cried. "But I daren't."

Then suddenly the back door of the room was thrown open. Both men whirled. There, in bedroom slippers, with a kimono thrown over her nightdress, stood Leda.

"Charley!" the girl cried, and with a little run threw herself into her brother's arms. "Why didn't they tell me you were here?"

"They couldn't," the man choked. "I—I—didn't want you to know—yet."

"I must wake up Bud," the girl cried happily, and dashed out of the room.

Leda had awakened quite suddenly, and for a minute or so had been unable to comprehend what had wakened her. Then she realized that it was the hum of voices from the front room. Her first thought was that Nancy must be talking to somebody. Then she remembered that she had heard Nancy go up to bed long ago. Her senses told her, too, that it was much later than Nancy was likely to be up. Then, as she became more awake, she realized that it was men's voices.

Suddenly she had sat bolt upright in bed, with her heart quivering so violently that she mechanically clasped her hands over her breast. Some vaguely familiar sound was purring in her ears like the memory of a half-forgotten tune. She couldn't place it, but its haunting familiarity drove her to her feet. She had moved across the floor and opened the door a crack. The low, rumbling voices in the front room came to her more plainly.

For a minute she had stood there in her white nightdress like a frozen statue. Then a gasp escaped her lips and she flew across to the stand and lighted the lamp. Dim though the voices were she had known that her brother was in the house.

"Well, sheriff?" the ex-outlaw asked hopelessly.

"No use rushin' matters," the sheriff said. "Just tell 'em that yo're helpin' me round up the Wild Ones."

Harrison had just time to give the sheriff a grateful glance when Leda entered the room, followed by Bud, who gave a welcoming whoop.

The sheriff left them together.

Sheriff Wendall was far more worried about Chet Kelvin than he was about the Harrisons. He was aware of the great risk his new assistant had run in returning to Codd's place. He was up early the next morning, hoping to get a sight of Chet before he walked down the street to announce his resurrection from the dead. But he was anything but prepared when early the next morning he saw Bill Codd himself waddling down the street toward Nancy Gemmell's premises.

"You folks keep out of sight," he told the others. "I've got a hunch that Bill Codd hankers after a private powwow with me."

"The nerve of that fat beast comin' tuh my house!" Nancy marveled.

Wendall met the man at the door. "Come in, Codd," he invited.

"Yes, I will—all outa breath," the man wheezed. "Have tuh set down."

"Help yoreself."

"Got somethin' here I s'pect belongs tuh you, sheriff," the man said, and unrolled the officer's vest with the badge.

"Yes, that's mine," Wendall said. "Where's the man yuh got it from?"

"That's what I'd like tuh know," Codd said. "The feller had the cold-brass nerve tuh want me tuh pay him for murderin' you. When I told him I counted you one o' my best friends he was some flabbergasted. O' course, I was afraid at first that he had murdered yuh till one o' my boys said he'd seen yuh comin' in here. But as soon as that feller saw I wasn't an enemy o' yores he jumped through a winder an' made his gitaway. His horses are still in my barn, but I don't know what's become o' him."

"That's a nice story, Codd, but I'm afraid yuh went too far," the sheriff said. "You murdered Chet Kelvin, Codd, an' I aim tuh see that yuh swing for it."

"You mean that you an' that feller tried tuh frame me?"

"Call it what you like, Codd, but if Kelvin ain't returned here alive in two hours I'll put you under arrest."

"That makes it hard, bein' misunderstood that way, but I guess I'll jest have tuh bear my cross," the fat scoundrel said lugubriously. "But I might remind yuh that yuh ain't got one single bit o' evidence against me. Well, I guess I'll be goin'."

He heaved himself to his feet and took a long look around.

"Nice place Nancy's got here," he chuckled, and waddled back down the road.

The sheriff called Charley Harrison and Nancy into the room. "I was fool enough tuh let Kelvin risk his life last night on the chance that we could scare Codd into talkin'. Now, if Kelvin ain't already dead, he's in a plumb desperate pickle."

"Hush! Don't let Leda and Bud know," Nancy cautioned.

"There's no use tuh look for him here," Wendall said. "There's just one chance. I had every trail outa town guarded last night. They must have taken Chet out of town and some of my men must have seen him go. What about it, Harrison— do you come out in the open with me now?"

"I'm with you," the man said shortly.

In less than an hour Wendall had ascertained that only one party had left town during the night. Two of the ranchers who composed the posse had stopped a light wagon in the night, but the driver had told them that he was loaded with supplies for the I X L.

"There's no doubt in the world that Chet Kelvin's body, dead or alive, was in the bottom of that wagon," the sheriff said. "There ain't much chance we kin do him any good, but we're headin' for the I X L."

TWENTY-THREE

CHET KELVIN had recovered consciousness before he was loaded into the light wagon, but he also found himself effectually bound and gagged. He could distinctly hear the conversation of the men who were bundling him about like a bale of hay.

"That damn' sheriff'll have the roads watched, so I'll git under the tarp with this feller till we git safe outa town," one man said.

Chet heard the driver of the wagon being challenged by somebody, but he was unable to move or make a sound. Soon after that the man called Tandy, who was with him in the bottom of the rig, crawled out and joined the driver.

It was, he judged, past midnight when the wagon stopped at the I X L. His head ached abominably, for the rough ride on the hard boards had been sheer torture. Presently the thongs which bound his feet were cut, and he was helped out of the wagon. There were three or four men around him, and they talked in whispers.

"Git him away from here right now," excitedly whispered a lean, lank man with an immense floppy old hat on his head.

"What on airth was Bill Codd a-thinkin' of? If ole Nevader wakes up—"

"Keep yore shirt on, Adam," Tandy rebuked. "Bill knows what he's doin'. Squash-head an' Uintah Jack can take him on from here. No danger o' them two turnin' gentle if he lets out a few groans."

Chet sensed that he must play for time. When they planted him on the ground he let his knees buckle and fell to the ground.

"Don't stall, feller, because yo're gonna take that ride," Tandy hissed. "If yuh can't set in the saddle yuh'll take it with yore head an' heels both a-draggin'."

"Fetch him into the house, boys. Mebbe a shot o' whisky'll bring him around a lot," Adam Broome urged.

Chet was half carried, half dragged into the house. There the gag was taken out of his mouth, and he was handed a tin cup half full of whisky. The fiery liquid did him good. He straightened up and looked the men over contemptuously.

"So you're Adam Broome," he addressed the owner of the floppy hat. "Ain't they told you that Bill Codd has been caught so he can't squirm, an' that you'll hang too if anything happens tuh me?"

"Don't worry about that, Adam. This jayhawker had Bill fooled fer a little while, but he had no more sense than try tuh fool him again after Bill got word who he really was. All Bill's gotta do is tell the sheriff this feller tried tuh hire out as a killer, an' when Bill was gonna turn him over tuh the sheriff he got scared an' run. Nobody's gonna know where he run to," Tandy said.

"I don't wanna git mixed up in it," Adam Broome protested weakly. "Take him away from here—an' I don't even wanna know where he's goin'."

"Fine," Tandy grinned. "Squash-head, you an' Uintah Jack put this hombre on a horse an' take him tuh the Red Water hole. You'll find Bobo, Tony, an' the Peace River Kid already there. Just give Bobo this note from Codd an' it'll tell him what tuh do. But if you lose him on the way yuh'd just as well pick out the likeliest tree an' hang yoreselves, because it'll shore happen to yuh anyway."

An evil-looking fellow with a flat, yellowish face came forward with a wide grin. Chet knew at once that he was a mulatto.

"Leave it ter us, boss," he said.

Uintah Jack proved to be no less disreputable in appearance than Squash-head. He, obviously, was part Indian. They had certainly picked a pair who were not likely to have their sympathies worked upon.

The rest and the whisky had invigorated Chet so that he felt almost normal, save for the terrific aching of his head. He realized that there was no use to offer resistance. He was in the most perilous situation he had ever faced, but he refused to give way to despair. There was still a chance that the sheriff might be able to do something, and it was possible that Kirk Holliday himself might interfere to save his life, though that was highly improbable. But he knew that Waite had been told not to murder him until Holliday was heard from.

His chief hope was that he might again take advantage of some error on the part of his enemies. But he couldn't force the issue. He must wait.

In less than an hour from the time he had arrived at the I X L he was riding away from the place between his two new guards. His hands were securely tied behind his back, and his feet lashed together beneath his horse's belly.

Daybreak found him in a region as rugged as that around Stag-tail butte, and as barren as the painted hills around Highriver. Noon found him on the edge of a dry, bleak desert. Evening brought him to a small water hole which gushed unexpectedly out from under a twenty-foot cliff of red sandstone. This, he knew, was his destination.

The appearance of the broken upheaval surrounding the spring was such as to turn any casual wayfarer from it. It was, Chet sensed, an ideal hiding place. The eager horses hadn't quite reached the water when Bobo Waite, the Peace River Kid, and Tony Mex stepped out from behind the cliff. Pregnant with danger though the situation was, Chet noticed that the Peace River Kid carried his right hand in a sling. Tony Mex had apparently recovered from his hurt.

"Well, I'm damned if it ain't our range detective—trussed up like a chicken," Bobo Waite said with a wide grin. "Where'd yuh git him, Squash-head?"

"Bill Codd he done sent him ovah—special delivery," Squashhead laughed. "Heah's his instructions."

Bobo Waite read the note and swore.

"Why the hell did he wanta drag Holliday into this? We coulda dealt with this hombre—plenty."

"Like yuh did at Stag-tail butte, huh?" Chet taunted deliberately.

"Yuh'll never git a break like that again, feller," Waite said savagely. "Well, roll him off, boys, an' bring him around tuh the tent. I reckon we'll have tuh endure him at least twenty-four hours before we kin hear from Holliday."

Chet was given no such latitude here as Kirk Holliday had allowed him when he was a prisoner before. His hands were untied only to let him eat; all weapons were kept carefully out of reach, and at least three of his five guards were always within a rod of him.

It was a little past noon when Uintah Jack, occupying the lookout post, reported that a single horseman was coming.

"He's comin' from Stag-tail an' his horse looks all in," the man reported.

In a few minutes, Chet knew, his fate might be decided. The vicious Squash-head was left in the tent to guard him while the others went outside to interview the newcomer.

Almost immediately Chet heard Bobo Waite's voice raised in angry protest.

"Holliday is crazier than a locoed sheep," the man bellowed. "I don't care if his damned draft was honored. He made Bill Codd believe he was an outlaw named Cherokee Fisher an' tried tuh git Bill tuh hire him tuh kill the sheriff. An' then him an' the sheriff tried tuh git Bill."

"That makes no difference," replied a steady voice, which sent a wild thrill through Chet's brain. "Kirk is plumb convinced that it would raise all manner of hell with the Wild Ones if anything happens to him, so he sent me tuh git him."

The speaker was Jack Fossum.

"He musta been in a hell of a hurry the way yuh rode that hoss," the Peace River Kid sneered angrily.

"He knew he couldn't trust yuh buzzards very long," Fossum retorted.

"Mebbe he's right," Bobo Waite said wickedly. "I never did like him, an' I never liked you. I believe yuh've been in with him all the time. I don't believe Kirk Holliday sent yuh. If he did it's gonna be just too bad, because Kelvin ain't goin' back— an' neither are you."

Chet believed that Jack Fossum had risked his life in a desperate attempt to save his, and now it seemed they would both lose. But to let Jack be shot down without making any effort to do something about it was unthinkable.

During the colloquy Squash-head had stepped to the front of the tent to listen. Chet, with his hands tied, was a few feet behind him. Chet had silently risen to one knee. Now he saw that for the moment Squash-head, though resting both hands upon his guns, was totally engrossed with what was going on outside.

Now, no sooner than Waite's threat had left his mouth, Chet shot to his feet and hurled himself like a cannonball at Squash-head. The top of his head struck the fellow squarely in the small of the back. With a yell of pain the mulatto fairly flew through space. He came down upon his face, but as he fell he collided with the back of the Peace River Kid's knees, and that worthy went over backward with another yell.

Chet, unable to stop the impetus of his charge also went down on his hands and knees. But the unexpected sight of the

124

big mulatto soaring through space, together with his wild yell, had caused the other outlaws momentarily to turn their attention from Jack Fossum to him. And Fossum was quickwitted enough to take advantage of the situation. His hand streaked to his gun, and he gave a quick leap backward just in time to evade Tony Mex's hands as that killer reached for him.

"Git 'em up, you sidewinders," Fossum hissed. He crouched dangerously, his gun moving from one to another of the discomfited outlaws as they paused with weapons half drawn.

None of them had the cold nerve to finish the draw in the face of that leveled gun. One by one their hands came up.

By that time Chet had scrambled to his feet, but the other two who had fallen were still down. Suddenly the Peace River Kid rolled over behind Squash-head and went for his gun with his left hand. The next instant the toe of Chet's boot, driven with terrific force, caught the outlaw on the point of the chin. It broke the man's jaw and put the Peace River Kid entirely out of the picture.

"Back up alongside the others," Fossum ordered Tony Mex. Then he made Squash-head get up and take out his knife.

"Cut them thongs on Chet's wrists," he directed, "an' if yuh so much as draw a drop of blood on him I'll let yuh have a bullet right in the guts."

A moment later Chet was a free man. He picked up the Peace River Kid's gun, and holding it in one hand he unbuckled the outlaws' gun belts with the other and let them fall.

"Tie 'em up hard an' fast, an' then we must git their horses an' travel," Fossum said.

"We're takin' 'em with us, Jack," Chet said.

"Hell, man, we can't do that," Fossum said. "Listen: Holliday didn't send me tuh bring yuh back. Him an' Blackie Payne, Sonora Yates, Hurricane, Al Biggers, an' George Tandy, an' two or three more are on their way here right now. I got out o' comin' with 'em by pertendin' tuh be sick, an' I like tuh rode my horse tuh death gittin' here ahead of 'em."

"But didn't Holliday git that money?" Chet demanded.

"Nary a cent. Hurricane come back without it."

This was something Chet couldn't understand, but he could appreciate the fact that the outlaw leader would be perfectly willing now to carry out the threat of execution he had once imposed.

"Just the same, Jack, I'm not leavin' here without takin' these murderers along," Chet said firmly. "I do appreciate you riskin' yore life tuh save mine, but if yuh don't wanna stick, their horses are out here just a little ways. Take one an' punch a hole in the scenery while there's still time."

Without a word Fossum strode out to get the horses. While

he was gone Chet compelled Squash-head to tie the hands of the others, and then he performed the same office for the mulatto. Only the Peace River Kid still slumbered.

Fossum saddled the horses while Chet worked to revive the broken-jawed outlaw. He had made up his mind that he would take the outlaws in with him, or not go at all. The idea of leaving such men as Bobo Waite at large to continue their career of murder and thievery was intolerable.

"Well, better hang him on a saddle horn by his belt so we kin travel," Jack said, as he came over and looked down at the prostrate Kid.

"I'm not askin' yuh tuh stay, Jack," Chet said quietly.

"I'm stayin'," Jack answered. "Since I've got in this deep I reckon I'd just as well touch bottom."

He turned and walked to the top of the highest cliff, but he didn't stay long.

"I guess none of us'll be leavin' here for a while," he remarked quietly. "Holliday an' his bunch are less'n a mile away. Any way we tried tuh leave now they'd nail us."

"I guess the tables are turned after all," Bobo Waite said sardonically.

"But it won't do you any good, Bobo," Jack Fossum taunted. "Yuh won't be able tuh sneak away this time an' leave us tuh face the music."

"Right you are, Jack," Chet laughed. "We've got just one chance that I can see. That is tuh hold the water hole till thirst makes 'em pull out."

He quickly outlined his plan—one which the outlaws themselves had doubtless already figured out in case they were ever attacked at the water hole.

The cliff just back of the spring was almost square on top, covering perhaps three square rods in all, and there was a natural parapet of sandstone almost surrounding it. The remainder of its surface was dotted with bayonet rocks the size of a man's body which had resisted the forces of erosion. There was a single, narrow trail leading up from the spring to the top.

The prisoners were forced up to the top, and while Chet guarded the men Jack hurriedly carried up such provisions as could be used, and filled several utensils with water. The outlaw camp was just behind the cliff, but it had little strategic value.

"Now let 'em come," Jack said grimly. "We got water an' they ain't. An' if we git thirsty we kin send one of these buzzards down after water. If somebody plugs 'em we at least won't be no worse off."

TWENTY-FOUR

WHILE the sheriff's posse was gathering in front of Nancy Gemmell's place that intrepid Amazon was getting into her riding habit.

"You don't mean to say that you're riding with the posse?" Leda said.

"As far as the I X L I am," Nancy declared. "If Adam Broome knows anything about this business, I'll git it out of him."

"Then I'm going too," Leda declared. "I couldn't bear to be left behind anyway with Charley going along, and—and Chet in such danger." She had quickly found out the truth.

"Kinda fooled about that Chet boy, wasn't yuh?" Nancy said.

"I never did believe that he was an outlaw at heart," the girl maintained. "I—I—couldn't bear to have him murdered."

"That's all right—he won't be," Nancy said. "But you stay right here. This posse'll have tuh ride hard an' fast, likely, an' yore brother an' the sheriff won't want tuh be bothered with wimminfolks."

It was only at the insistence of Charley and the sheriff that Leda consented to remain behind, and it was even harder to persuade Bud to stay with her. Nancy assured them that she would be back before noon.

The posse had been gone no more than half an hour when Leda suddenly missed Bud. The last she had seen of him he had been watering Snip and Coley. She rushed out to the stable, and to her dismay discovered that the black pony was gone. In defiance of orders, Bud had followed the posse. She was all alone on the place, save for the helpless old Leppy.

For a moment the girl hesitated; then she ran into the house and changed into her riding habit. She had no saddle, but she knew that she could ride the Snip horse bareback. As she ran out the back door she confronted a man, who silently handed her a note. She frantically read:

"Dear Miss: If you don't want any harm to come to your brother you'd better call on me." That was all.

"Who wrote this?" she gasped.

"Better see Bill Codd," the man said laconically. "He kin tell yuh more about it than I kin."

With blind fear clutching at her heart she turned and ran up the street to Codd's hotel. In response to her inquiry she was directed to the fat man's private office. She found Bill Codd wedged comfortably into his chair.

"What have you done with my brother?" she demanded.

"Which brother?" Codd asked coolly. "The kid or the outlaw?"

"You know which one I mean," she shot out angrily. "And what do you mean, 'outlaw'?"

"Set down," Codd ordered. "You ain't gittin' anywhere with me by puttin' on airs. I'm wise about this scheme tuh steal the I X L."

"What do you mean?" Leda gasped.

"Just what I say. I know that infernal sheriff let yore sweet-scented brother outa the pen tuh put up a job on me. Thought they'd git somethin' on me so I couldn't defend myself, an' then make a bluff that he'd bought the I X L. Well, they can't git away with it. I reckon they'll bump into more trouble than they kin assimilate anyway, but if they don't they'll either leave me alone or they won't see you or yore kid brother again."

"Do you actually mean to charge that my brother has been an outlaw?" she demanded in a steely tone.

"Good Lord! Is it possible you've been fooled about that? That precious brother o' yores is known here as Dude Johnson, an' he was sent up for twenty years for train robbin'. They only let him out so's he could help frame me."

For a moment Leda's heart seemed to die inside her breast. Much as she detested and loathed the fat man, she felt that he was telling the truth.

"What do you want me to do?" she asked brokenly.

"Yo're gonna take a trip us Highriver, sister, to a place where there's only one way out. If yore friends are reasonable, nothin' will happen to you. But if they ain't—it'll be jest two steps an' a tumble into the river."

The next moment Leda felt herself grasped from behind. A rag was jerked around her mouth and tied tight. She was hustled down a steep trail to a break in the gorge through which the river ran. At the foot of the trail she found Bud weeping with helpless rage.

They were mounted upon horses, and then to Leda's astonishment Bill Codd himself came down the trail, mounted upon a little roan pacer. It was Chet Kelvin's roan.

The only man who accompanied them besides Codd was an Indian, whom the saloonkeeper addressed as Ammon. It was a tough and somewhat perilous trail they followed, several times having to cross and recross the river, but the Indian led the way with the assurance of familiarity.

Despite the easy gait of the roan Bill Codd soon began to groan. The man showed every evidence of relief when they paused at the mouth of a small cave which faced a narrow ledge which, as Codd had said, was just "two steps and a tumble" from the river.

"I'm stayin' here with yuh, an' don't think because I'm fat that I kin be fooled with," Codd said. "There's two parts o' this cave. One opens on the river above here, but the only way out is back this way. You kin have the other part, but don't try comin' back this way without callin'. An' yuh couldn't git away anyhow till Ammon comes back with the horses."

Leda had long since worked the gag under her chin. "We're not foolish enough to get ourselves killed, but I think you'll find the law will make you pay for this," she declared.

"That'll depend on who makes the law—me or Jay Wendall," Codd said. "Take the horses back, Ammon, an' do just like I told yuh. No matter how much they threaten they don't dast do nothin' for fear of what'll happen tuh these kids."

It was insufferably hot even so early in the day, and the fat man wiped his perspiring brow with a big silk handkerchief and hastened to seek the shade. Leda and Bud went into their compartment of the cave.

"What do yuh think?" Bud asked anxiously.

"I think we'll be all right," Leda replied bravely. "All we've got to do is wait. As soon as the sheriff and Charley rescue Mr. Kelvin they'll come an' get us."

"That Indian'll never tell."

"No; I suppose not," Leda admitted. "That's why Codd himself came up here. He was afraid they'd force the truth out of him if he tried to face them. He isn't much used to punishment. But I'm not going to give up. Our friends will find a way."

"I wish they'd hurry," Bud said.

Long before Leda and Bud had reached their stopping place, the posse had arrived at the I X L. Adam Broome put in a reluctant appearance, and at sight of Nancy Gemmell his sloping shoulders seemed to droop more than ever.

"Where's Chet Kelvin, Broome?" the sheriff demanded.

"Where's which?" Adam countered.

"You know what I mean. Chet Kelvin was brought here in that democrat wagon over there last night. We want him."

"Yo're mistaken, sheriff," Adam said. "That was jest a load o' supplies."

"You lie," gritted the sheriff. "I've got plenty on you, Broome. If you don't wanta face a murder charge too—talk."

"But I tell yuh—"

"Let me talk," a voice broke in, and old Nevada stepped to the front. "I ain't been a derned bit pleased at havin' tuh stay yere, but I ain't had no chanc't tuh git away yit. But las' night when this wagon druv up I was awake. I dassn't leave the

129

bunkhouse, but I did look through the winder an' I saw 'em liftin' a man out. An' a while atter that I saw three horsemen ridin' away. But only two men was missin' from here when the others come back tuh the bunkhouse. That was a mulatter they call Squash-head an' a breed named Uintah Jack."

"Now what have yuh got tuh say, Broome?" the sheriff challenged.

"I don't know a single thing about it," the man replied.

"Sheriff," Nancy Gemmell said grimly, "I'm askin' yuh tuh arrest that man for the murder of my husband, twenty years ago. He told me with his own mouth that he tolled my husband to his death, an' that there was a letter which Martin wrote after he was shot which accused Adam Broome of shootin' him. Bill Codd got the letter, but I can prove by the dyin' statement of an outlaw named Jap Walton that Adam Broome—"

"I didn't kill Martin—honest tuh Gawd I didn't," Broome broke in. "Nancy, yuh promised not tuh—"

"I promised not tuh use that confession unless I had to," Nancy said grimly. "This is a case of have to. Unless you tell us where they took Chet Kelvin the sheriff'll have tuh arrest yuh."

"An' yuh'll have tuh go with us so we'll make sure yuh ain't lyin'," the sheriff said.

"I'll tell," the unhappy man said miserably. "I reckon it can't be no worse than bein' Bill Codd's dog all these years has been. They took him tuh the Red Water hole."

"All right. Git yore horse and come on," the sheriff said. "We may be in time yet."

"Do I go along?" Nevada asked. "I ain't gonna be right welcome here no more."

"No; you go back tuh town with Nancy here," the sheriff said. "I ain't been feelin' just right about leavin' them Harrison kids alone there nohow."

"My God, sheriff, you don't think Bill Codd will dare—" Charley Harrison burst out.

"I don't know. He's an old sidewinder, an' if he got scared enough he'd do most anything. But I reckon they'll be all right till Nancy gits back, an' even Bill Codd would have a time doin' anything to 'em with her on the job."

It was a grim, silent, hard-riding posse that pursued its way toward the Red Water hole. Even the sheriff didn't know where it was located, and the other members of the posse, except Charley Harrison and Adam Broome, had never heard of it. They were all aware that they might be riding into a trap, and even if they succeeded in surprising their foes, they realized that they might be too late to help the man they hoped to rescue.

130

They knew that they couldn't reach the place much before dark and even if they could it would be unwise to approach in daylight. Their one chance, as Charley Harrison explained, was to make a surprise attack.

"If they see us they'll hold us away from the water hole till we have to retreat," he explained.

"An' we're gonna need water plenty bad," said a posseman by the name of Jim Nelly. "Lord, but it's hot. An' look at them thunderheads hangin' on the mountaintops back yonder toward the head o' Highriver. If there ain't some cloudbursts over there this afternoon I miss my guess."

"If it wasn't fer Nancy Gemmell," said a pious member of the posse, "I bet the Lord would have sent a cloudburst big enough tuh wash Highriver off the earth long ago."

Some five miles from the water hole the posse came to a halt behind a knoll to rest their horses and to wait for nightfall. There were eleven men in the party in all, and the sheriff had no hesitancy in letting the two former outlaws, Harrison and Broome, carry arms.

For several hours there was a constant dull roar of distant thunder, but only a few drops of rain fell upon them—not enough to relieve their discomfort. They were all eager for darkness to come so they could be on their way. It had been hours since their horses had had a drink, and the men's canteens were empty.

"It's allus good policy tuh take 'em on two sides," Sheriff Wendall said. "Harrison, you take five men, an' come up from the far side. Me an' the others will crawl in as close as we kin, an' be ready fer action as soon as we hear yore signal."

"That being the case I think we'd better separate here so we can make a wide circle," Harrison suggested.

"All right," the sheriff agreed. "It's dark enough now, so let's be travelin'."

With Adam Broome and the three other men by his side the sheriff rode slowly toward the water hole. The other party, having farther to go, would travel faster.

It seemed that they could have been little more than half way there when they heard firing.

"Great grief!" the sheriff exploded. "Them boys must certainly have rode like the mill-tails o' purgatory tuh come on 'em so quick. Come on, men—for Gawd's sake ride."

Unaware that the shooting they had heard had been done by the Wild Ones and Chet and Jack the men galloped forward. And while they were doing so, the other party, making the same ghastly mistake was charging straight into the water hole—firing, not at the Wild Ones, but at the two heroic defenders of the cliff.

TWENTY-FIVE

KELVIN and Fossum had no more than had time to get themselves established before the party of Wild Ones was in full view. There were nine in all—and every one a fighting man.

"This ain't gonna be no snap, Chet," Jack Fossum grinned. "I hope I don't have tuh shoot old Biggers. He's an awful fool an' he's bad clean through, but I'm kinda fond of him."

"Let's hope we don't have tuh shoot any of 'em," Chet said. "I think we'd better powwow a little."

When the outlaw party was a hundred and twenty yards from the water hole Chet fired a rifle shot into the ground ahead of their horses. They came to a sudden, surprised stop.

"Who the hell fired that shot?" Kirk Holliday yelled angrily.

"Me—Chet Kelvin. Just a little signal for yuh not tuh come any closer. This water hole is pre-empted."

They could plainly see the consternation on the outlaws' faces.

"I don't give a damn who you are—yuh can't keep us away from that water hole," Holliday called furiously.

"I'm not foolin' with yuh, Holliday," Chet retorted. "Yuh'll have tuh stay back. The first man who comes a yard closer will git a bullet."

"What's the idee?" the outlaw chief demanded.

"Just this: I wasn't a law man when I was around yuh before, but I am now. I've got Bobo Waite, Tony Mex, an' the Peace River Kid up here, an' I'm takin' 'em in as prisoners."

"Mind tellin' us how yuh aim tuh pull off that little job—single-handed?"

"Not a bit. I aim tuh hold this water hole till you fellers have tuh pull out. Then I'll take my prisoners an' go."

"We're not lettin' yuh take any prisoners anywhere, Kelvin, an' before we leave we mean tuh let yuh know what we think of spies," Holliday delivered his ultimatum. "Yo're crazy if you think you can hold off a bunch like this."

"You'll be crazier if yuh try comin' any closer to me."

The outlaws turned suddenly and spurred their reluctant mounts away from the water. They quickly disappeared in an arroyo.

"Hell's shore gonna pop around here," Jack shrugged.

"Looks like they meant business," Chet admitted. "We hold the water hole, but they'll git all the horses. Even if we drive 'em away they'll leave us afoot. We'll be in a tight box unless Jay Wendall picks up our trail some way."

"For once in my life I'd be almost tickled tuh see that old coot," Jack murmured. "Hey, look!" he broke off.

The outlaws' horses, sans saddles and blankets, but wearing hopples, were crow-hopping into the water.

"We can't shoot horses," Chet said. "All we can do is try tuh keep the men thirsty. But it shore looks like they meant tuh stay a while."

Bobo Waite laughed discordantly.

Jack Fossum at that moment raised up a bit too far to look around. Wham! A rifle ball tore the top of his sombrero half off and splattered upon a rock behind him.

At frequent intervals then came single shots and occasional volleys from all sides. The Wild Ones were closing in.

Several times the defenders replied to the shots when they thought they saw a man move, but without any luck. They realized that their foes meant to keep them annoyed, while staying out of sight themselves, until it grew dark. Then they would make a try to reach the water.

Dusk settled rapidly around the water hole, and though a handicap to the besieged men in some ways, it was an advantage in others. Now they could see the flash from every gun fired at them, and by being constantly alert they were able to return the fire with much better effect.

Jack was the first to make a hit. Firing at a return flash, he brought forth from his antagonist a bellow like that of a roped bull calf.

"Was that you, Biggers?" he yelled. Long before that Bobo Waite and the others had yelled out the information to the outlaws that Jack Fossum was the traitor who helped to oppose their entrance.

"No, it wasn't, but when I git my hands on you I'll break every bone in your carcass," called back Jack's former partner.

There was now a constant hail of bullets from all sides and they spatted against the rocks with a menacing plunk. The top of the cliff reeked with the pungent odor of powder smoke and the tang of rock dust. Twice Chet felt the drag of bullets through his clothing, and a chip of rock drew blood on Jack's face. The five prisoners hugged the ground in a warm embrace, the while they breathed anathema against their captors.

The outlaws were still using rifles, but the defenders, because of the necessity for quick shooting, were relying altogether upon their short guns. Thanks to their prisoners, they had a complete arsenal. Chet was watching the side next the water hole, while Jack had the other. The former's position was the more dangerous, for every instant he risked being shot in the back.

Suddenly a man leaped from behind a boulder, and made a swift run toward the water. Chet aimed low and pulled the trigger. The way the man collapsed showed that he had been hit in the leg. For a few minutes he writhed upon the ground in agony, then he began to slowly drag himself toward the water hole. They let him crawl on undisturbed.

"The next man who tries that will git it higher up," Chet called.

"Don't be a fool, Kelvin," Kirk Holliday shouted. "We've got yuh treed. We can send a few men back for water if we have to while the rest holds yuh there."

"Better send 'em then," Chet called grimly. He saw something dark moving upon the ground. He had to watch it carefully before he knew it was a man crawling toward the base of the cliff above the water hole on his belly. All the time Holliday was telling him how crazy he was.

Chet took deliberate aim at the ground just in front of the squirming figure and fired. It filled the crawler's face with sand. The fellow jerked back; then snapped a shot at the cliff. The next moment he was rolling over and over toward the water. Again Chet fired, and this time the man lay still. That man was George Tandy—possibly now in the bosom of Abraham.

There was a temporary lull in the fighting, and the two besieged men gratefully mopped the sweat off their perspiring faces and grinned across at each other.

Ten minutes later the outlaws savagely renewed the attack at closer range, with their six-guns, plainly hoping to make it so hot for the two on top that they would have to keep their heads down. It was the supreme effort of the Wild Ones.

It was keep down or be killed. Once Chet thrust his gun around a bayonet rock to take a blind shot, and the weapon was shot out of his hand. For five minutes his wrist felt as if it had been broken, though his skin wasn't scratched.

Always they were obliged to keep an eye on their prisoners. Even tied men may be dangerous, as Chet himself had demonstrated. Chet had turned to look at them when he suddenly saw Tony Mex raise his head. The next instant there was a squashy sound, and the man's head went down as if it had been hit with a hammer. The killer had cheated the gallows after all. Tony Mex had got a bullet in the brain. Luckily for the defenders, it transpired, for in some way the fellow had got hold of a knife, and was in the act of cutting Bobo Waite loose when he was hit.

134

At the risk of getting a bullet through the head, Chet peered between two rocks, and saw a man running away from the water hole, carrying a bucket. He started to fire, but a bullet smashing against the rock within three inches of his face filled his eyes with rock dust. He missed. He heard a groan from Jack.

"Git you, pardner?" he asked anxiously.

"Some," was the game reply. "But never mind me."

Facts had to be faced. The outlaws had got enough water to enable part of them to hold out until some of their number could bring water in kegs from some other water hole. And there was no escape for the two on the cliff. But in Chet's mind was no thought of surrender.

It had been cloudy all evening, but now the clouds had floated away and a whole canopy of stars blossomed forth in silvery glory. There came a sudden volley of yells from the south, and the two on the cliff were amazed to see half a dozen riders charging in wildly from that direction.

"Give 'em hell, sheriff!" one man whooped loudly.

The firing toward the cliff ceased abruptly. That is, the men who had been firing stopped, but the newcomers were blazing away wildly at the already bullet-riddled cliff.

"What the hell?" Jack cried.

"It's a posse—but they think we're the outlaws," Chet said. He yelled out at the top of his voice, trying to put the posse straight, but the din was too great for him to be heard or understood.

The posse was within a hundred feet of the water hole when the outlaws opened fire. At the first volley a man reeled in the saddle and plunged headlong on top of a sagebrush. It was Charley Harrison!

With wild yells the other five turned and galloped away. Having heard the firing, they had made the same error as the sheriff, and believing that the other party had attacked before the signal they had made a premature charge.

"Grab yore horses, men!" yelled a voice which Chet recognized as Kirk Holliday's. "There's another posse comin'."

Chet leaped to his feet, and reckless of danger, plunged down off the cliff. His one thought now was to grab Kirk Holliday before the famous outlaw leader could get away. The Wild Ones were running toward their hoppled horses, which had fled some distance from the water hole when the shooting started. Soon Chet found himself practically among them, but not so close but that they supposed him to be one of themselves.

Holliday was the man he was after, and he paid little attention to the others. Suddenly he saw a man spring up after removing the hopples from a horse. It was Holliday. As the man leaped to the animal's bare back Chet fired, but a whirl of the horse caused him to miss. But he had attracted attention to himself. He dropped to the ground as Holliday fired, and the outlaw's bullet whizzed over his shoulder.

They were a good hundred yards apart—too great a range for accurate shooting with a six-gun even in daylight. Holliday's plunging horse made him a difficult target, but the man seemed disposed to want to come to closer quarters. They blazed away at each other several times without effect, and then the proximity of Sheriff Wendall's party caused Holliday to change his mind. With a yell at the remnant of his followers he galloped madly away.

The battle was practically over. The Bobo Waite gang were still prisoners. Two outlaws, George Tandy and Tony Mex, had been killed; two others, Sonora Yates and the fellow called Hurricane, had been too badly injured to travel. Hurricane was the man Chet had shot in the leg while trying to reach the water hole. On the other side, Charley Harrison was dead and Jack Fossum had a badly wounded arm.

"Well, Kelvin," Sheriff Wendall said, "you've helped me achieve the biggest ambition of my life. I've got the Waite gang, an' all I've got tuh do is put the screws on Bill Codd, an' I'll be rid o' that fat bloodsucker."

"But Holliday got away," Chet said disgustedly.

"Don't worry about that," the sheriff chuckled. "We couldn't have convicted Holliday of anything in this county nohow, but one thing he won't never be able tuh live down here is the fact that he was whipped so bad he had tuh run away without his saddle. Don't worry, we won't be troubled in this section with the Wild Ones for some time tuh come."

"About Jack Fossum?" Chet queried.

"I never wanted him very bad or I wouldn't have had Dude Johnson turn him loose when he was arrested before."

"It's not goin' to be very pleasant, sheriff, telling Leda and Bud that their brother is dead," Chet murmured.

"No, it ain't," Wendall said. "But now that he is gone I can't see no use of tellin' 'em anything worse than we have to. It won't do no harm, I reckon, tuh make 'em think that he was workin' for me all the time, an' never was an outlaw."

"Thanks, sheriff," Chet said earnestly.

"I think, though," the officer said, "that I'll just go through his pockets tuh make sure there ain't nothin' there tuh make me out a liar."

A brush fire had been built beside the water hole, and everybody had collected there. The sheriff straightened up

136

with an oblong packet in his hand, and gave a startled exclamation. He tore off one corner.

"Twenty-five thousand dollars!" he exclaimed. "Where in thunder did he git that much money?"

"I kin tell yuh that," spoke up the outlaw called Hurricane. "The lousy cuss took it offen me. It was the money I got on that draft Kelvin made out. He laid for me, an' I dassn't tell Kirk the truth, so I said the draft was no good."

"So he was a crook to the end," the sheriff murmured.

"Wait," Chet said as the sheriff handed him the packet. "This package is addressed to 'Leda Harrison, Saratoga, New York.' He took the money, all right; but he didn't do it for himself. I'm sure he intended to go straight if he could get out of here."

Almost Chet found himself wishing that the girl could have got the money; even though it would have brought ruin to him.

"We'll just lay by here tonight an' hit the trail back in the morning," Sheriff Wendall said, and presently things grew quiet around the Red Water hole.

It had just turned day when someone yelled that a lone rider was approaching. It proved to be old Nevada. He had ridden all night.

"What's up?" the sheriff demanded.

"It's them young Easterners I brung inter the country," Nevada said. "Bill Codd has got 'em."

"What?" Chet cried.

"Yes, sir, he's tuk 'em an' flew. An' he left word that if the sheriff wanted tuh save their lives he'd have tuh make terms that suited Bill Codd."

"Why, I'll fry the grease outa his fat carcass—"

"Yuh'll ketch him first, sheriff," Nevada said. "He left word that the go-between would be that Injun, Ammon. An' yuh couldn't git nothin' outa that redskin with two fires."

Chet Kelvin was already picking up his bridle.

"Hey, where you goin'?" Jack Fossum asked. "Don't yuh know we ain't had breakfast yet?"

"To hell with breakfast," Chet said rigidly. "I'm on my way."

"An' I'm right with yuh, son," said the grim, tough old sheriff.

TWENTY-SIX

NEVER in his life had Chet made a harder forced ride than the one he was now on. He and the sheriff had commandeered the two best horses, and they rode without mercy. When Chet had been taken to the Red Water hole from the I X L ranch the trip had required sixteen hours to make. The return journey was made in a little less than half that time. They changed horses at the I X L, and ten hours from the time they had started they drew rein in front of Nancy Gemmell's place.

"Any news, Nancy?" the sheriff asked.

"None," the old woman answered. "All I can git outa that outfit is that Bill Codd himself took 'em somewhere an' give orders that that Injun, Ammon, was tuh talk tuh nobody but you."

"Then I'll go see him," Wendall said. The grizzled officer's face was gray with fatigue, but his will was still indomitable.

"Wait, Jay," Nancy urged. "Yuh can't force nothin' outa that Injun. Yuh'll have tuh make terms."

"Make terms nothin'," the sheriff growled. "I'll take him by the windpipe an' tear the truth outa him."

"No," Chet protested. "If he won't talk willingly we'll buy him if we can. I've got twenty-five thousand dollars in my pocket. I'll give every dollar of it if necessary tuh find out where they are."

"We'll see," the sheriff mumbled. "But I won't make terms with Bill Codd."

They had little difficulty finding Ammon. He scarcely looked up as they approached.

"See here, you," the sheriff blustered. "We wanta know where Bill Codd took that boy and girl. If you don't tell—"

"If you do tell," Chet interrupted, "I'll make it worth yore while."

"You give me glass-eyed horse?" the Indian demanded surprisingly.

Chet hesitated but a moment. "Yes, I'll give you the horse."

"He took 'em up river yesterday," the man said. There was a peculiar, sardonic grin upon his face.

"Then you lead us tuh the place," the sheriff ordered.

"Sure. I lead you to the place," the man said as he rose. "Findin' bodies—that your job."

"What do you mean, yuh rapscallion?" Wendall demanded.

"Bill Codd make me leave 'em on river bank, under bluff. No can git away on account river. Yesterday come up big storm in hills. Cloudburst. Sweep down river gorge mebbe twenty feet high. Look."

The fellow pointed down toward the river. They remembered the mighty thunderheads they had seen hanging upon the mountaintops the day before. Now they saw that the river was still a turgid mass of thick, yellow water. The lines

138

of fresh débris on each side of the gorge showed how high the water had reached. They knew that any creature caught ahead of that foul flood would stand no chance whatever.

"You—you—mean—to say—that Codd and—and the others were caught in that?" Chet cried jerkily.

The Indian shrugged. "No could git away," he replied.

Truly, Chet thought, the Harrison family had come to a tragic end through the weakness of one who had yielded to the lure of outlawry. Not only had he met a violent end himself, he had brought his sister and brother to destruction. And in that tragic moment Chet knew that something had gone out of his own life which could never be replaced.

"All right," he said evenly. "Git some horses. We—we'll look for the bodies."

The sheriff went along, but he was soon left behind as Chet urged the Indian to greater and greater speed. There was small chance that the bodies would ever be found, but the sheriff paused to look into every pile of drift.

The sun had gone down when Chet and his guide splashed across the river for the last time, and Ammon pointed out the place where he had left the party. Chet could see that the water had reached far above the cave, and in receding had left it clean.

And then, suddenly, a joyous yell burst upon his ears. Bud Harrison appeared at the entrance of the cave, and his sister was just behind.

"Thank God," the cattle buyer breathed while something strangely pleasant gripped at his throat.

"We knew you or Charley, one would find us," Bud shouted.

"How—how did you ever escape?" Chet gasped.

"See that little ledge o' rock down there just above high water mark?" Bud demanded. "We just did manage tuh make it tuh there, an' clung up there for hours with that dirty water a-lappin' against our feet."

"And Codd?"

"He couldn't make it," Bud said soberly. "The storm was over, an' all at once we heard a kind of a grumblin' roar. We didn't know what it was at first, an' then I remembered what old Nevada told us about cloudbursts in this country. I yelled to Codd, but I hadn't any more'n got the words outa my mouth till we seen it comin'. Gee, the front of it was ten feet high right above the river. I could see big boulders as big as a house just bein' picked up an' tumbled along. An' there was a kind of a sound like a growlin' bulldog makes, only as much louder an' bigger as thunder is to a gun report. It—it—just kinda froze a feller's whole insides."

"An' then what?" Chet prompted.

139

"Then Leda she saw that ledge an' screams for us to run for it. We just did make it. We could hear that fat man pounding along behind an' beggin' us tuh wait for him, but, gee, we didn't have time."

"Oh, it was horrible," Leda said. "I looked back just as we were climbing the ledge and I saw Codd coming. His face was ghastly. He was trying so desperately hard to run, but—but he was too fat. And—and then"—the girl's face became pale with the memory of what she had seen, and she gave a shudder—"and then I saw the flood right behind him. Something came down from the top like—like a giant hand reaching out to get him. I couldn't bear to look. When I looked again he was gone."

It was enough. In his mind's eye Chet could picture the terrified fat man's futile race with death. It was something to try to forget.

"Never mind that now," he said tenderly. "We'll soon be out of this."

They met the sheriff half a mile down the gorge, and before it was really dark they were back at Nancy Gemmell's. Three kindly conspirators agreed to say nothing to Leda and Bud about their brother's death until the next day.

"And don't say more'n yuh have to till after I have a talk with Adam Broome," Nancy said. She explained her plan with great animation.

"You bring it off, an' I won't arrest old Adam," the sheriff said. "He's only been a cat's-paw anyway."

The posse and the prisoners arrived the next day. Leda and Bud had to be told of their brother's death. Chet and the sheriff undertook the task while Nancy Gemmell corralled Adam Broome in her living room.

To Chet's relief Leda received the news calmly. Bud was of course, badly broken up; but already he was getting great consolation from the fact that Charley had died a hero. Presently Bud went out, and then the girl's attitude changed.

"It's awfully kind of you to try to save Charley's good name," she said evenly. "I'm glad of it—for Bud's sake. But you needn't try to deceive me. Bill Codd told me the truth. I know that Charley was an outlaw."

"But he changed his wild ways, an' he died fightin' on the side of the law—don't forget that," the sheriff said.

"I'm not likely to," the girl replied. "It's the one thing that makes it bearable."

It was at that moment that Nancy walked into the room. Unaware that the girl knew the truth, Nancy blurted: "Well, dearie, we can't bring yore brother back tuh life, but we can restore his property tuh you. The I X L is in Adam Broome's name, but Adam Broome admits that he's got no right to it, an' he's willin' tuh deed it to you today."

"I—I—don't know why you are all so kind to us," Leda half sobbed, "but we can't take anything—knowing what Charley has been."

"She knows," the sheriff said.

"Well, somebody's gotta take it," Nancy said. "It don't belong to Adam Broome, an' Bill Codd is dead. If Leda won't take it, then I'll make old Adam deed it to Chet Kelvin."

"Me?" Chet exclaimed.

"Why not?" Sheriff Wendall demanded. "If it hadn't been for you this country would still be overrun by outlaws. You've earned it an' there ain't a thing against yuh takin' it over."

"But I just happened tuh be here," Chet expostulated. "If it hadn't been for Leda I never would have come here."

"There you are," Nancy cried triumphantly. "They're both of 'em entitled to it. Come on, sheriff, le's let 'em talk it over."

There was an embarrassing silence after the others had gone.

"Why did you say you wouldn't have come here if it hadn't been for me?" she asked finally.

"That slipped out, Leda," he confessed, "but I'd just as well tell the truth. Maybe I didn't realize just what it meant at the time, but when I saw what you was up against in comin' in here I just had tuh trail along tuh try and protect you. I reckon you know why."

"So—somehow I've felt all along that I could depend upon you," she confessed.

"They want tuh give us this ranch. We can't either one take it alone. Shall we—take it together?"

"It would be heaven for Bud," she murmured.

"But what about you? Do you hate it so much?" he asked.

"I'd love it, with you," she whispered. He leaned toward her, but she held him off with the palm of one small hand pressed against his lips.

"I want you to know," she said softly, "that the ranch doesn't make any difference. Wherever you asked me to go with you I'd go."

"Bother the ranch," he laughed. "We'll turn that over tuh Bud an' Jack Fossum, Nevada, an' even old Adam Broome. But just as soon as it can be arranged you an' me are goin' on a honeymoon."

A small, restraining hand was brushed aside. It didn't resist much anyway.

THE END